Advance praise for Embracing the Dark

In embracing the unknown, and making of it an art, the writer of horror fiction confronts the greatest issues that have plagued humanity since prehistory. Eric Garber has brought together a selection of shuddery winter tales that are meant to entertain, but which inescapably provoke. These tales invite us, in the safety of our easy chairs, to ponder the endless night that awaits within all of us.

—Jessica Amanda Salmonson
author of *The Encyclopedia of Amazons*
and editor of *What Did Miss Darrington See?*

❑

In assembling these leave-a-light-on tales of the unnatural, Eric Garber has done a great service for fans of fangs and guys (and gals) who are into ghosts. It's a bloodly wonderful collection for any reader who believes chills up and down the spine are hot.

—Richard Labonté

EMBRACING THE DARK

edited by **Eric Garber**

Boston: Alyson Publications, Inc.

Typeset and printed in the United States of America.

This is a paperback original from Alyson Publications, Inc.
40 Plympton St., Boston, Mass. 02118.
Distributed in England by GMP Publishers,
P.O. Box 247, London N17 9QR England.

This book is printed on acid-free, recycled paper.

First edition, first printing: November 1991

5 4 3 2 1

ISBN 1-55583-167-2

COPYRIGHTS

Contents

Acknowledgments

Many thanks to Allan Galanter, Rebecca McDuff, Lyn Paleo, Tim Williams, and Scott Winnett for reading stories and sharing suggestions.

Many thanks to Sasha Alyson for his patience.

And, of course, thanks to Jeffrey Sunshine, for the title, the week in Provincetown, and more.

Introduction

Most of us enjoy getting scared. As children, we huddle in the dark, telling each other spooky ghost stories. As adults, we thrill at riding roller coasters, stand in line for hours to view Hollywood's latest horror thriller, and anxiously await Stephen King's latest blockbuster. These hair-raising amusements are cheap and fun. They deliver a safe, controlled way to deal with dangerous and frightening emotions like fear, disgust, and rage, and they offer a quick escape from the very real horrors of disease and violence that surround us. At their best, they tease the subconscious, stirring primal passions and innate fears.

There is a growing and devoted audience for these unsettling creepy thrillers. High-tech monster movies like *The Exorcist, Alien* and *Friday the Thirteenth* pack motion picture theaters across the country. Luridly packaged paperbacks, bearing titles like *The Urge* and *The Coven,* are national bestsellers. Their appeal is to the gut, not the intellect. They do their best to scare the wits out of their audience.

Unfortunately, with a few exceptions such as Clive Barker, Anne Rice, and Michael McDowell, horror writers seem overwhelmingly misogynous, antisex, and homo-hostile. While some of their mass-market amusements are subtle studies, the majority are clichéd potboilers drenched in gore and violence. The standard horror novel glorifies heterosexuality. A virile male, representing the Good, the Pure, the Christian, and the Patriarchal, battles an unspeakable monstrous depravity, representing the Evil, the Profane, and the Sexually Chaotic, to save a feisty, but ultimately helpless female, representing Heterosexual Love and the Family.

Most horror writers punish any deviation from this heterosexual norm. Thus, in John Skipp and Craig Spector's "splatter punk" thriller *The Light at the End* (1986), a closeted gay man is cruelly raped by a blood-thirsty vampire, and in James Herbert's *The Rats* (1974), a self-hating alcoholic homosexual is eaten by hundreds of rampaging rats. In Charles Panati's *The Pleasuring of Rory Malone* (1982), both lesbians and gay men are brutally assaulted by telekinetic powers.

In fact, numerous horror writers have explicitly linked homosexuality to the very evil threatening their heterosexual protagonists. The unholy vampire in Ron Dee's *Blood Lust* (1990) is a bisexual man, who sexually butchers both sexes. The progenitors of a lethal microbe in Harry Adam Knight's *The Fungus* (1985) are lesbian separatists. In Ray Russell's *Incubus* (1976), a loathsome demon brutally assaults a string of women, only to be revealed as a lesbian. The ugly metaphor is obvious: homosexuals are immoral, doomed, violent monsters.

The eleven horror and dark fantasy stories in this collection are very different. They reject the cliches and invert the metaphors. Gay men and lesbians are at the center of these delicious tales of the macabre and the horrible, and not as helpless victims. There is humor, and sex, and suspense. Some of these stories are touching and warm-hearted. Others are disturbing and scary. Many use the traditional horror stereotypes in new and exciting ways, creating an out-of-the-closet generation of vampires and werewolves. Several deal directly with the contemporary nightmares of child abuse, racism, rape, and AIDS: the true terrors of our technological age.

These stories signal something new from the ancient musty mausoleums of horror fiction. Love and community can now be found among the moonlit shadows. Desires long stigmatized as evil, blasphemous, and ugly are finally being given their due. These stories celebrate their difference. They welcome the night. They embrace the dark.

Works of Art
Nina Kiriki Hoffman

Sally was sitting on the artwork again. For several minutes she didn't notice I was home. I watched her perching on one branch and caressing another, her eyes closed, her face serene. I felt an ache in my belly that had nothing to do with menstrual cramps. She already loved the artwork more than she loved me; how was she going to survive its destruction? How was I?

The artwork was the first thing I saw every night when I came home from being an accountant and opened the door to the apartment. We had taken all the furniture out of the living room to make space for it. Cerveza, the artist, installed it himself; it had to be brought in pieces and reassembled. It was pale wood, the kind advertisers call blond, and branchy — twisting limbs going this way and that, rising from a central point on the floor and spreading up and out. To really appreciate the thing you had to climb around on it and study all the carvings. Some of them I could recognize — a face here, a bas-relief of a crane in flight there — but many more seemed random designs. Some of the carvings were in narrow crevices between limbs and could not be seen, only touched. When we first got it, I spent a lot of time with the artwork too; shapes from it printed themselves on my dreams. I found myself doodling them on scratch pads at work. When I rubbed my eyes, I stopped seeing little purple stars; I saw a field of carved faces or an Escher-like checkerboard of birds turning to clouds. During my thrice-weekly workout at the gym, started since we got the artwork, I imagined shapes pressing against my palms as I lifted weights; I felt hand-carved information speaking to the soles of my feet as I pedaled the Exercycle.

I perceived the artwork in bits and pieces. But Sally, ah ... Sally, who worked at her loom at home, tried to tell me about the work's Gestalt — how it all fit together, a tree of life, the story of the evolution of consciousness, the growth of the ability to dream. She wove more trees into her tapestries, and other shapes I recognized from the artwork. And her weavings got better; she had better gallery showings, and sold more tapestries. "Art, like a chromosome, needs to replicate," she said, "to create its own copies and spread out where it can reach everyone and transform them. Heisenberg had it backwards. The experiment exists only to affect the observers."

Half the time I didn't know what she was talking about. All I knew was that I loved her, whatever she said and did.

"Lucy," she said, when she finally noticed me standing by the front door that night, "come and feel this. There's a sequence here—" She twisted between the limbs, ducked under the branch nearest the front door, grabbed my hands, and pulled me into the embrace of the artwork.

We eeled our way over and under branches to the far corner of the room, where we had once kept an aquarium. Like a teacher at a school for the blind, she took my hand and placed it on the underside of a branch. A rounded dome swelled against my palm. She moved my hand inward along the branch toward the core of the tree, and I felt a dome punctured. I explored with my fingers and realized a spiral started on one edge and wound its way to the heart of the dome. Again she pushed my hand to a swelling on the branch. I felt a curled pattern — the dome spiraled and chambered like a nautilus.

"Now," said Sally. She pulled me away from that branch and put my hand against the central trunk. I felt a concavity under my hand. I closed my eyes and pressed my fingers into it. Was it the shape of a bi-lobed brain, or a four-chambered heart? The divisions were so subtle.

"Do you understand?" she asked.

I felt like a blind student asked to make an intuitive leap. Dome. Spiral. Chambered spiral. Brain. "No," I said. I no longer wanted to understand the artwork. Cerveza sold it to us two years before; it cost us Sally's large legacy from her grandparents and the whole of my IRA, minus penalties for early withdrawal. By now Cerveza must be almost finished with his next piece, and just before he completed it, he would come to us to fulfill the final clause in the contract. Only one finished Cerveza piece ever existed at a time. He believed that to balance the creative and destructive energies, he must destroy each of his creations. "What if I created and created, never destroying anything?" he had said at a lecture Sally and I went to, back when we still held hands in public. "What if each of my creations were better than the last? I would be making a vortex, sucking all the creative energy out of the cosmos around me, and a balance of destructive energy would fill the resultant vacuum. Who knows? If the work were great enough, the destructive energy could express itself in another war! So, always, I balance the use of the energies."

Sally understood his lecture, or said she did. When we bid on the work at auction and captured it, she spoke with Cerveza, saying his integrity impressed her and she would cherish the artwork even more, knowing its ephemeral nature.

Since we got it home, she had been developing theories of her own — as had I. "The artwork," she said that night, "the artwork is about evolution. What is evolution but higher orders of organization? Energy organized in increasingly complex ways. The defeat of chaos. So maybe there is a balance, but it tilts. Why shouldn't there be two Cervezas at once?" She jumped up on one branch and briefly hugged another. "Proliferation—" she said, waving at the branches, which rose from a central trunk, to spread and fill the upper part of the room. "Expansion. He's telling us, through this, that his focus has changed. If we put more creative energy out into the environment, maybe it can send the destructive energy away. If destruction feeds on itself and grows, why shouldn't creation? Isn't it time we tipped the balance the other direction?"

I took her hand and kissed the palm. I loved her enthusiasm, her intensity, her focus. She gave me a smile and touched my cheek.

"I bought artichokes," I said. I glanced over my shoulder toward the front door, where I had abandoned my bag of groceries when she led me to her discovery.

"You darling," she said, and tugged a lock of my crimped hair. I had been trying different hair colors for the past two years. Just now it was ash blonde, pale as the artwork's branches.

"You like?" I said.

"The best yet. Suits you."

"I got another tattoo."

She looked distressed. She didn't understand why I started getting tattoos — another recent habit. I knew sometimes in bed she found herself fascinated and excited by them, and she felt ashamed later. All these things she did not say aloud, but her body spoke to me.

"Where is it this time?" she asked.

I rolled up my sleeve and showed her the gauze bandage on the inside of my left forearm. "A phoenix," I said, "four colors." I smiled at her. She would be curious, waiting for the scabs to heal, wondering how skillful Deadeye Dick had been this time. There would be an itch in her that might coax her attention away from the artwork for a little while, and bring her focus back to me. And that would be good. "I'll go cook supper now," I said.

She nodded. She stood on a branch and reached up for the one above. She closed her eyes and stroked the branch, searching for the hidden meanings

❏

Cerveza's call came four days later.

"Can we meet you for tea somewhere?" Sally asked. I watched her face as she listened to his reply. Her blue eyes narrowed, then widened, tear-bright. "No, I—" she said. A pause. She bit her lower lip. "You don't understand. Your art cries out to be preserved."

She waited. She squeezed her eyes shut and tears spilled out. When she opened her eyes, she stared at the ceiling, twisting the phone's coiled cord around her wrist and pulling it tight. "Denial," she whispered. "Very well." She hung up the phone as though it were an egg and might crack if mishandled.

"Oh, Lucy," she whispered.

I went to her and offered what comfort I could.

When her sobs slowed, she said, "He's coming tomorrow morning, with an ax."

❑

I woke, showered, and called in sick.

In the kitchen, I stared at a tapestry Sally had made me before anyone knew her work: an olive green artichoke, its leaves slightly open at the top to show the tiniest fuzz of violet from its flowering heart. "You're like that," she had said to me then, two months before we moved in together. "This beautiful flower, this colored fire, locked inside prickly leaves."

I loved her for seeing me that way. Everyone else had touched the prickles and backed away.

I stroked the silky weaving. How carefully she worked. This wool came from Iceland, and had a sheen and softness all its own. She dyed it herself, using natural substances. She called this art forth, as if a person could spin yarn from clouds — she the spindle, summoning wool from her subconscious, spinning it into a solid thing she could weave and shape. That a person who had so much inner fire could look away from herself long enough to see and treasure the fire in me had never ceased to amaze me.

I drank a glass of orange juice and went to the living room.

Sally had spent the night climbing over the artwork. "He said naturally I must mourn it," she told me when she had calmed enough to eat supper. "Of course I want to deny that it's going. He didn't even want to hear my theories. He said everybody tries to talk him out of doing it, but he knows what he believes. So if you don't mind, Lucy, I'd like to spend this last night — studying it, as much as I can."

Of course I didn't mind.

She had come to bed at last, exhausted, just at sunrise.

I went to the core of the artwork and hugged one of its branches. It seemed to be made just for me to hug — smooth, warm, knobbed with bumps that fit perfectly into my embrace. Against my stomach I felt a shape, printing itself on my skin. After a moment I let go of the branch and knelt to see what the shape was. An embryo so young I couldn't tell what species it might be.

I went to our bathroom and stood studying myself in the mirror. In two years I had firmed and perfected my figure, following a body-building regimen at the gym that always demanded a little more of me than I wanted to give, until I remembered why I wanted to give it. A small green tattooed frog sat like a jewel on my right hip. A rose opened red petals around my navel. The phoenix on my left forearm had healed into beauty, and a snake curled around my upper right arm like a bright bangle.

My pale crimped hair hung down to my shoulders. I made a thin plait on the left side, threading three brass beads into my hair weaving. Should I add makeup? My face looked pale, in concert with the rest of me. No. After two years, I was finished. I smiled at myself, satisfied with the work I had done.

I put on the red robe Sally had given me for my birthday. Then I went to the living room, to huddle against the artwork's trunk and wait for Cerveza.

The morning light was chill in the room. The artwork looked like bones in the touch of the cooled sun. I wondered whether my plan would work, whether I wanted it to work.

A knock sounded on the door. Sally cried out in her sleep. I got up and opened the door for Cerveza.

He was a tall man, rough and grizzled, with long earlobes and a high bulging forehead. His eyes under his out-thrust brow looked dark and precious, jewels in a crevice. His mouth was broad, with deep brackets on either side of it. Black and gray stubble forested his chin and cheeks. He wore a green coverall and carried an ax.

I stepped out into the hall and closed the door.

"What is it?" he asked. His voice had a comforting rumble, like a sleepy hive of bees.

"I want—" I said. "I've worked—" I looked at the ax. It looked old and used, its head darkened with age, though the blade shone in arcs from a recent bout with a whetstone. The wooden handle looked smoothed and oiled with the sweat of palms. "Does it have to be *your* art?"

"What?"

"Suppose you destroyed someone else's art? Would that make it all right for two of your pieces to exist at once?"

"I have no right to anyone else's art. And if it isn't good enough to make up for the new one, what use is it?"

I felt a chill in the pit of my belly. It would be so easy to open the door and let him in, and his ax with him. Listening to Sally sobbing for days and nights afterwards, though — that would be too hard. "But if it is good enough, and if it's offered to you freely?" I said.

He looked at me for a long moment. He blinked.

I straightened. I let the robe slide to the floor, and stood, feet planted firmly, my hands outstretched before me. "This is what I have," I said. I looked down at the slope of my breasts. I glanced at the phoenix on my arm, its blue and green tail feathers and wings outspread. I clenched a fist and the muscles of my upper arm bulged. "What a piece of work..." I looked up at him again.

"Mine to destroy?" he said. I did not understand the tone of his voice. It had a curious waiting flatness in it.

I nodded.

"All right," he said.

"I just want to leave her a note," I said.

"No." He leaned his ax against the wall and pulled my robe up around me. "Come," he said, retrieving his ax and taking my arm.

His studio was in a warehouse, windowless and huge. In the center of it was the work in progress, carved limbs again, but this time not a tree; it was a skeleton, if a human skeleton had had the stature of a dinosaur; and it was like an unfinished house, a framework without walls or roof; and even as I thought these things, made these labels, I noticed something that made the labels lie — no one thing, just a final detail that made the images wrong. I walked to the artwork and touched it. Its surface was rough and abraded; my fingers brought away splinters.

I looked at Cerveza.

"You are greater than anything I could create," he said. "I wonder I didn't think of this before. How it hurt me to kill all my children ... what is your name?"

"Lucy," I said. My throat felt dry. "Lucia Vanessa Nike."

"Luvani," he said. "I will name this one after you."

But it's so ugly, I thought. I wonder if Sally would understand it. I thought of the fresh pain of the tattoo needle, the ache in my arm after Deadeye Dick finished my phoenix.

I thought of Sally's beautiful face, her contented smile as she sat on the artwork, the joy she got from discovering something else about it. That piece deserved to live — more, I thought, than this one did. Cerveza could name this one after me, but I thought of Sally's piece as mine. I remembered the press of the embryo shape against my stomach. What species?

Artwork.

How many mothers could choose their children?

I leaned back against a splintery limb and watched, smiling, as Cerveza raised his ax.

Blood Relations
Jeffrey N. McMahan

Sorting the mail, I stop short when I read the return address of the gilt-edged, perfumed envelope. Guilt impales me. The rest of the mail drops to the floor; I drop onto the sofa. The childhood address burns my eyes; my mother's perfume stings my nostrils.

Guilt.

Andy, I haven't heard from you in ages.

Guilt.

Andy, your cousin finished *his education.* He *doesn't have to work in a clothing store.*

All this guilt chews at me before I've even cracked the scarlet wax seal graced with Father's family crest. I tap the end of the envelope against my teeth. I could traipse through eternity without letters from my mother filled with tidings of guilt and everyone else's good fortune.

Buck up, Andrew, I chide myself, your fortune isn't so bleak. So I'm dead but still kicking. So I carry an onyx-handled switchblade with which I cut off my drained mark's heads. So I sleep in a coffin during the day. Things could be worse...

Nights like this make me wish that my death had gotten better publicity. If everyone thought me dead, I wouldn't have to deal with mothers and that lot.

Even the undead have unrealized dreams. I died in my bathtub at the teeth of a leather-clad Vietnamese stranger who was just passing through town. No obituaries for Andrew, thank you very much. I just got back up and went about business as usual — with minor alterations in my schedule and diet.

Resigned to the inevitable, I tear open the end of the envelope. The letter, as if possessed of its own will, slips out of the envelope and unfolds in my hand.

Dear Andy—

The woman gave me the name Andrew, why can't she use it?

I don't understand why you never write. Your father says you must be dead.

My father — knows all, tells nothing except when not asked.

Drawing in a breath of courage, I forge on. It seems there's a family gathering in the future. My uncle's sister's mother-in-law is on her deathbed.

I will call when Hattie has breathed her last. You must jump on the next plane. No excuses, Andy. Funerals are the only time we all get to see each other nowadays.

How macabre, a funeral reunion. Those Lyalls are such innovators.

❏

The telephone rings. I nearly drop my strawberry margarita. All evening, an itch in my brain has foretold that the two weeks of silence following Mother's letter wouldn't last. I toy with my glass. The ringing continues, reminding me of summons when I was a child. Gulping my drink, I cross to the phone.

"Andy?" the moment I pick up the receiver.

"Ma, what a ... surprise."

"Don't call me that. Why haven't you called? Aunt Hattie kicked ... Aunt Hattie has passed on."

Nice cover, Ma. "I never thought she'd go."

She instructs me, "The minute we hang up, you are to get on the next plane here."

"Ma, that might not be so—"

"You mind me, Andy ... Everyone expects to see you. Even your cousin Paul is flying in."

Cousin Paul? I remember a scrawny kid about thirteen. Make that twenty-three; I haven't seen him in ten years.

"Answer my question, Andy."

She asked me something? "I would be extremely upset if I missed the funeral." Especially since I never had one of my own.

"Land's sakes, Andy, don't you ever listen to your mama? We'll be expecting you." The line goes dead.

I gape at the receiver. Why, Bobbie Estelle Grant Lyall, what a Georgia drawl you have!

Mother tries so hard to be uptown, but she can't shake a taste for 'possum stew. Ma's country stock with a southern leaning, kinda the farmer's daughter marries the millionaire whose family has seven hundred years of recorded English history. She wants Winston — the Fourth — and me to be uptown, too. Winston is in: he finished law school. I, on the other hand, am the Great Disappointment. I didn't finish college. I sell clothing to pay my credit card bill. Moon above, what would Ma say if she found out I'm dead?

❏

I live in California, my parents in Connecticut. Vampiric wisdom says don't fly into the sun. I catch the first after-dusk flight and hope for good tail winds. I can't land too close to dawn, or I'll get a sunburn the likes of which my mother has never seen.

Not having a fold-away coffin, I am forced to leave mine at home. I keep a plastic bag of soil for such occasions. There is an old — if cramped — cedar chest in my bedroom at the old homestead that had done coffin duty more than once.

"Steward, why are we still circling over the airport?" I ask, torn between the twirling lights below the wing and the man collecting plastic cups. "It's getting rather late, isn't it?"

The steward leans close. "We should be landing within the hour," he assures me. "There was a heavy snowfall. They're still clearing the runways." He motions at the other passengers, snoring in blissful ignorance of our plight. "We don't want to disturb anyone, now do we, sir?"

I glance out the window for signs of dawn on the horizon. "Within which hour, did you say? Tonight or to-(gulp) day?"

❏

A rude taxi drive dumps me on my parents' doorstep. Before me stands the home of my humble beginnings. With forty-odd rooms, Lyall Manor, as Ma likes to call it, is a modest affair of brick, white marble columns, and stained glass — too reminiscent of a cathedral for my tastes.

After dragging my luggage up twenty thirty-foot-wide steps, I fumble in my carry-on for my keys. Dawn is fast approaching, and Andrew cannot afford to be locked out.

The front door swings inward. I'm struck with a blast of warm air and blinded by bright light.

"Lose your key again?" my elder brother's voice demands.

Shielding my eyes against the glare, I make out Winston's gaunt figure on the other side of the threshold. A woman lurks behind him. "That your new skirt?" I inquire.

"'Drew!" Winston chides.

Does *anyone* in this family know my name?

"Help me carry this stuff in, and I'll be nice."

Winston and I struggle the suitcases inside. His fiancée gapes at me as if she's never seen a real person before.

"Come through to the drawing room," Winston says. "Drink or coffee? Veronica made fresh."

Let Veronica keep her fresh to herself. And tell her to quit licking her lips at me. She's making me jittery.

"I'm exhausted," I reply, smiling over Veronica's head.

"Andeee?"

No rest for the undead.

Mother swirls into the room. The dim, multicolored light from the Tiffany lamp does her well. I could be ten, and she could be swirling in to chide me for dying Winston's blond hair blue. Her blonde hair is perfectly coifed around her thin face, her green eyes perfectly mascaraed. Not a wrinkle flaws the nightgown flashing beneath her open silk dressing gown. She must sleep standing before her vanity.

"You should have telephoned, Andy," she greets me. "I would have sent a car to get you."

"And how are you, Mother?"

"Your room is made up." She drills me with a look of damnation. "And spotless. The maid said there was mud all around the cedar chest after your last visit."

"I'm tired." It's almost dawn. "Keys." I extend my hand.

She pinches up her face. Reluctantly, she digs a key ring from the pocket of her dressing gown. "Why you need to lock—"

"I want to sleep. We don't keep the same hours." I mock her drilling look of damnation. "You won't give me any privacy."

"Winston doesn't lock himself in when he sleeps."

I glance at my brother, Veronica leering at his side. The remarks I could make would straighten the beauty-parlor curls on Mother's head.

❏

"Glad to see you've risen from the dead," my father greets me when I enter the dining hall the next evening. I falter. My father, Winston Lyall III — that tall skinny person passing as my brother is Winston Lyall IV — has always unnerved me with his acute instincts.

I offer a cryptic smile to cover my unease. Years of experience have taught me not to humor my father too much — it brings out the best in him. The man has a snide tongue; I've never heard anyone like him.

"When's the big funeral?" I ask, taking my usual seat at his right elbow. I pour wine from a crystal decanter and kick back for the traditional one-on-one with the Old Man. "Gee, don't tell me I missed it."

"We get our last gander at Aunt Hattie tonight and plant her tomorrow," he replies, intent on his *sausage en brioche*. "Food's not half-bad. I've barred Estelle from the kitchen."

"And I was hoping for collard greens." I cast about the room just in case Mother is listening.

Father hasn't changed a great deal from my blurred childhood memories of him. His dark hair is still thick and wavy, longish at the collar. Although he is seated, I can tell that the eldest of the lanky Lyall frames has been kept in prime condition. He's a lawyer and likes to impress jury members with his svelte self.

"How's the clothing business?" he inquires.

"Colorful," I reply, adjusting my label. "Fashion is such a fickle patron, though. If one isn't careful, one could find oneself overpowered by its influence while the rest of one's life goes to hell in a hand basket."

Father scans me head to toe, then grins ear-to-ear. For the first time in my life, I've elicited a genuine smile from him. "Let's hope that never happens to you, Andrew."

I knew I could count on him to remember my name.

Mother whisks into the room. She graces Father with a murderous glance. "Dearest, you are supposed to wait to eat with the rest of us." She tugs impatiently at the bellpull. "Ornery servants pay me no mind!" she snaps.

Whoa, Ma, tone down the chitlins accent, the neighbors might be listening.

"I'll have your *brioche* brought in, Andy." She smiles sweetly at Father's and my slack-mouthed expressions. "Winston and Veronica aren't joining us. We're to meet them at the funeral home." How quickly she composes herself.

"Andy, is that what you're wearing to the funeral home?" she asks, sneering at my ensemble. "It is a bit ... festive."

"He's a bit festive." Father hides behind his wineglass.

"I'm not into drab," I say, scanning her black-and-gray suit. "This is the best I can do."

She *tsks* through the dining hall to the kitchen door. It swings shut. After a moment's silence, she bellows at the maid to get the damned vittles on the table.

❏

Aunt Hattie's funeral is the largest reunion of the Lyall clan in Father's seven hundred years of recorded English history. Throw some streamers and balloons here and there — a tasteful array around the coffin — and we could all get down and party.

All the color, however, would clash with Aunt Hattie's plastic pallor. A foot or so from the coffin — just in case that dead look is contagious — I study the white face, black eyebrows and lashes, scarlet mouth, and rosy cheeks. Does Bozo work at this mortuary? For all intents and purposes, Aunt Hattie looks ready to sit up and juggle some lilies.

"You're smiling, stop it," Winston IV says, joining me.

"She's never looked more alive..."

"'Drew!" my brother chastises.

"...It's as if she's sleeping. I know she's going to open her eyes and crack that ruby mouth into a smile."

"You're an abomination," Winston proclaims, nose in the air.

"She does look horrendous," a male voice says from my other side. I face the eavesdropper. Be still, my dead heart. I didn't know there were certifiable hunks in the Lyall clan. "She never looked this bad when she was alive," he adds.

"She's dead, Paul," Winston whispers sharply. "She's not supposed to look like a beauty queen."

Paul does. So this is little Cousin Paul. How he has — I drop my gaze — filled out. Cancel the funeral, Andrew wants to crawl over Paul's terrain for a couple hours. Aunt Hattie's dead; she can wait.

"Your enthusiasm is showing, 'Drew," Winston sneers.

"Go find Veronica, Winny." I extend my hand to Paul. "It's been a long time, Cousin Paul."

"It certainly is — has," Paul says, wrapping his hot hand around mine. "You haven't changed at all, Andrew." He strokes my palm. "Your hands are a bit cold," he comments.

"Forgot my gloves," I reply. "You've changed." Beyond my wildest imagining. "What do you eat?"

"Andy..." Mother's voice calls.

"My mother possesses incredible timing," I apologize in the moment before she drags me a million miles across the room. Why do I suspect Winston put her up to this? She knows I have no interest whatsoever in Cousin Rachel.

❑

Paul displays an inordinate — and decidedly unhealthy — interest in Cousin Rachel. Should they be standing so close, their heads so inclined? This is a funeral, not an orgy.

Nonetheless, as I mingle with the relatives I notice that Paul's brown eyes trail me — like slaves. I like it, I could get into it — if, as he spoke, his hand didn't hover quite so near to Cousin Rachel's left mammillia.

I purposely pass in and out of range. Paul, the sly dog, manuevers Cousin Rachel into a slow spin as I circle the room. If nothing else, I have proven a fascination for him.

I'm getting dizzy from this wandering and from the confused impressions twirling in my head. I seek out the old folks, don my corpse facade, and complain of nausea. Mother buys it, even if she doesn't want it; Father gives me a look I recall from childhood. He assesses the gathering to pinpoint the cause of my retreat. By his smirk, he's on to me like Paul isn't.

En route to the door, we collide with Winston and Veronica. Mother explains my illness. Winston smirks —

not as well as Father. Veronica offers condolences — a few years too late.

"You're not leaving." Paul presses at my elbow; Cousin Rachel has been abandoned to Aunt Hattie's company. "I thought we would go out for a drink or something."

I kinda had that in mind, a quick one to slake the thirst and quiet the hormones. They are rampaging, especially with his hand brushing eversolightly against the back of my slacks.

Now I am confused. Is Paul torn between two cousins, or is he testing his bisexual wings? My vote's cast for wing testing.

"Andy feels nauseated," Mother puts in.

"'Drew's nausea is very severe," Winston embellishes.

"Andrew looks as if he's recovering to me," Father retaliates.

Father knows best.

❏

For a dead guy, I experience a miraculous recovery. Not that I could get sick; I am dead — immune to human disease in any shape or form. Germs and viruses and such find it difficult to get a foothold in dead meat.

Unfortunately, Winston IV thinks I have too fully recovered and invites himself along. By the shadow of Father's snide expression on Winston's face, he thinks I'm up to no good. So, for once in his life he's right, that doesn't mean I have to like the fact that he's going to ruin everything.

Paul, Winston, and I leave Mother, Father, and Veronica — and Cousin Rachel, thank the sunset — to the funeral festivities. As we pile into Winston's BMW, I wonder at how quickly these gents abandon their women for a night of drinking with the guys. I've tossed back a few with some women and have not found their drinking antics any better or worse than the guys I hung around with in my daylit days. Why are hetero men — and lest we forget, suspected wing-testing bisexuals — averse to female companionship on their drinking outings?

Too soon the answer to my queries looms through the windshield. Winston swings the BMW into a tiny parking lot beside a gaudily lit building. Andrew hopes his night vision is merely deteriorating, because he thinks that flashing hot pink neon sign reads, *Girls! Girls! Naked Girls! Rolling in Oil!*

"This is where we're having our drink?" I inquire. Now I am feeling nauseated. Watching naked women cavorting in oil is not my idea of a good time.

"We can go somewhere else if it offends your sensibilities," Winston offers — insincerely.

"If you had any sensibilities, you wouldn't have pulled in here to begin with," I retort.

"We'll make a deal," Paul intervenes. "If you get completely disgusted, we'll leave."

I am already completely disgusted that Paul is willing to make deals to get through the door. But I am the one who recovered for this foray; I may as well tag along.

After extracting promises on penalty of death to leave at my first visible gag reflex, we pile out of the car and wade through black, slushy snow to the dark interior of this fine establishment. We are greeted by flickering light, heavy smoke, and bestial bellowing. I curb an instinct to retreat. At my sides, Paul and Winston are already antsy with excitement. They can't find a table fast enough — ringside, of course, with a clear view of the oil-wrestling pit at the base of a five-foot stage where a languid woman laboriously sheds her garments.

"You boys been to a funeral?" the barmaid asks, dropping napkins onto the water-ringed tabletop.

"Aunt Hattie's," Paul replies, eyes glued to the stage.

"He serious?" the woman returns, her eyes shifting between Winston and me.

"Deadly," I reply. "How extensive is your drink menu?"

"How fancy you willing to go?" she parries, giving me the thrice-over. She's figured me out. The fact that I haven't looked at the stage but once and keep my eyes fixed to hers rather than on her breasts, where my gentlemanly brother's are glued, might have pegged me. She whispers conspiratorially, "I wouldn't go too fancy, these gents aren't very liberal-minded."

"Draft beer," I order, "or is that asking too much?"

"Borderline. You two?" She nudges the table to get Paul's and Winston's attention. "To drink?"

"Beers," they reply, then swing their faces back toward the stage as another dancer makes her entrance.

"Nice friends to bring you here," the barmaid says as she walks away.

Tell me, sweetheart. Blood relations; what's one to do but endure their repulsive foibles?

The lights dim as the dancer drags off her last stitch. A roly-poly man in a tight tux lumbers into a pin spot. He flashes a smile full of gold teeth as he announces the commencement of the oil-wrestling contest. "Any volunteers from the audience?"

The rowdy response to his announcement fades in answer to his question. As the barmaid sets up our drinks, I glance around. Not one of these sleazeballs is feeling macho enough to tangle with a bikini-clad muscle bimbo in a vat of Wesson.

"What do you say, Paul?" Winston blurts around a mouthful of beer suds.

Paul contemplates the blonde with the bazookas wading around the oil pit. Slurping down his beer, he shakes his mane of black hair, loosens his tie, and makes a quick swipe at his crotch. "Yeah ... I can take her," he replies.

"We got a volunteer!" our barmaid, eavesdropping on this unbelievable exchange, heralds. While the sleazeballs shout enthusiasm — and relief that they're no longer on the spot — the barmaid leans close to my ear. In a rush of hot breath: "Now we'll both see what's under that dark blue suit."

To my utter amazement, Paul stands up — he's actually going to go through with this. The barmaid sends him backstage. She then informs Winston that Paul's excursion into the realm of oil wrestling will cost him exactly one hundred dollars — eight-by-ten color glossies of the event included. Winston, unblinking, flicks the cash out of his money clip. I could buy a decent shirt and half a pair of pants for that.

"Another round of drinks," Winston says, "and a dozen tequila shots." He leers triumphantly to indicate that I was wrong about the wing testing. "We'll give Paul a good send-off."

The fresh round arrives before Paul emerges from behind the stage curtain. He wears a pair of too-large gray boxer trunks. The audience jeers and hoots as he briefly parades his wares; he possesses a bit more in the muscle department than most of the Lyall men. Paul climbs down into the oil pit.

"Paul!" Winston extends a shot of tequila over the railing.

Sloshing through the oil, Paul takes the shot and tosses it back. With a plastered smile, he winks at me. He turns to face his formidable opponent.

And they're basted! The weight-toned favorite flexes her sinewy body and pounces on Paul. His feet slip from under him. They plop into the oil, roll to the left, roll to the right. Paul doesn't stand a chance. Every time he scrambles on top, the woman flips him facedown into the oil. The only advantage I can see — I'm ensnared and craning for the clear view — is that all that oil has turned those oversized gray boxers into translucent nylon tricot that wetly molds to Paul's crotch and butt.

Paul manages a grip and heaves his opponent across the pit. Trying to gain his feet, he turns his back on her. She lunges. Her fingers trace four trails through the oil lacquering Paul's back and catch the boxers. Paul succeeds in standing, but the boxers don't follow and languish in the oil around his ankles.

Our barmaid, turned *paparazzi*, snaps off a roll in a series of blinding flashes. Obviously, she is as impressed by Paul's upstanding display as Andrew.

❑

By the time we depart *Girls! Girls! Naked Girls! Rolling in Oil!*, brother Winston is up-to-the-top-of-his-blond-head sloshed. I don't think sacrificing my share of tequila shots, plus my fourth and fifth beers, on his behalf had anything to do with it. Paul and I dump my brother into the Beemer's backseat. Paul closes the door on Winston with a slam of finality.

The two of us stand beside the car, flipping through the photos of Paul *a la oil*. The barmaid has quite the eye for composition, especially on those extreme close-ups. Paul divvies up the stack and hands half to me.

"Souvenirs," he replies to my astonished expression. He steps closer, pinning me against the car. What was drenched in salad dressing an hour ago rises to life against the front of my slacks. Paul shrugs inside his open overcoat, loosens the neck of his shirt. "Don't you think it excruciatingly hot, Cousin Andrew?" he inquires, drilling me with his narrow brown eyes.

"For ten below zero, excruciatingly," I reply, with more than words. My instincts are as sharp as my father's. Paul is about to test his wings to the fullest of their abilities.

❑

Winston's snoring in the backseat doesn't dampen the ardor Paul has worked up. Parked on a secluded road, shielded by steamed windows, Paul and I maneuver around the Beemer's stick shift and hand brake. We neatly stack overcoats and suits over the seat back and writhe flesh to flesh. Paul has tested his wings before; a novice doesn't reach this position on the first try.

"Are you cold?" Paul asks, reaching my face after a tongue tour from my toes. "Your skin is like ice." His second encounter with my lack of body heat sparks suspicion in his eyes.

I consider explaining that undead people rarely run a ninety-eight-point-six, but I don't think he would continue after that revelation. I cup my hands under his butt and seat him firmly on my lap. He tosses back his head, eyes shut, and grips my shoulders. I think I've driven suspicion from his mind.

The BMW sways with our passion. I recall visions of oil wrestling and burn with the satisfaction that I won the toss for Paul's attentions. I lower him onto his back, press my feet against the passenger door, and strive with purpose.

I lean closer; another fire ignites within me. My lips draw back from teeth sharply elongated and aching with lust. I experience a momentary dilemma. Paul is my .cousin, a blood relation; completely satiating myself on him will definitely cause a family scandal. But, as he is of my blood, I desire him from my core and must drink from his rapture. Maybe I can just sample a pint or two. I may not find it as satisfying as going all the way, but I really shouldn't leave my own cousin's bloodless corpse lying at a roadside.

I press my lips to his throat, my fangs pierce his warm skin, and the liquid of his life gushes into my mouth. Paul groans in sheer ecstasy. His hand cups my head, his legs clamp around my waist to secure our union.

"I was supposed to stop this kind of activity, 'Drew," Winston's voice slurs.

I turn to my brother peering over the backseat. Winston's face blanches; his bloodshot eyes dart between my face and Paul's blood-smeared throat. His mouth drops open, then works in voiceless terror. He gasps and spits out, "Andrew!" before his eyes roll back and he flops into the backseat in a faint.

❑

I awake to the sound of the telephone clamoring for attention. Pushing up the lid of the cedar chest, I unfold my body and rise. This thing could use another foot of length so a dead guy could stretch out his legs. Massaging cramps out of my rigored knees, I stumbled to the nightstand and pick up the receiver.

"Andy, you slept through the funeral," Mother greets me. "Winston says he isn't surprised. What happened last night? Paul looked like death itself this afternoon."

What happened last night ... How quickly every detail skitters through my brain. The evening wrapped quickly after Winston intruded upon my intimacies with Cousin Paul. After cleaning Paul up and dressing the two of us, I dropped Paul with his parents — giving an explanation of tequila shots, yet politely omitting details of Paul's wrestling inabilities. I drove back here, tossed Winston into his room, and folded myself into the cedar chest. That shouldn't be too hard to explain.

"Your father and I would like a word with you, Andrew," Mother says through the telephone. *Andrew?* Something tells me Winny has been watching too many horror movies and has placed the wooden stakes on the table. "We'll be waiting in the library. And don't dawdle, Andrew. Paul's family will be here soon for dinner and cocktails."

Paul will probably be able to tell some real chilling ones.

❏

The Family Lyall waits solemnly in the library. Winston IV, his pale eyes keenly set on me as I enter, stands ramrod straight by the fireplace. Winston III sits in a leather chair to one side of the hearth. He lifts a doubting-Thomas eyebrow at me. Mother lounges on the chaise opposite, a silk handkerchief twisted in her frail hands. Are the dim lights playing tricks on my night vision, or does Mother's makeup look streaked?

"Took your sweet time," Mother drawls, uncoiling the handkerchief. She scans my ensemble. "You look nice. I suppose working in a clothing store has its advantages."

"Go ahead and ask him," Winny prods our parents. His gaze meets mine, and he takes a backward step.

"Your brother has an … interesting … explanation as to why Paul looked so pale today," Father says. The corners of his mouth twitch, dying to curl into a smile. "Something to do with oil and teeth." An embryo of the smile appears. "He wanted us to call Monsignor Westerhausen and buy stock in a silver mine."

"Silver's for werewolves, brother dearest," I reply, giving Winny a derisive look.

"He admits it!" Winny shouts, jabbing a finger at me.

"Oh, Andy, honey," Mother says, her voice edged with Georgia. "That story Winny told us ... sweetheart ... darlin', tell your mama the truth now."

Poor Ma, all the highbred facades crumble under stress. I recall occasions of tearful self-loathing from the past when her slips into down-on-the-farm colloquialisms stopped many a blue-blood heart dead. I step toward her; she cringes on the chaise. I draw myself back.

"I'm dead," I state, looking at each of them. "I have been for a couple of years." I pin my gaze on Winny. "I'm a vampire, if you want the truth."

"We'll call Doctor Morgenstein," Mother says, nodding slowly. "He'll talk you out of this foolishness."

"Well." Father stands. But he can't decide where to go.

"I told you, didn't I?" Winny says, triumphant. "He was drinking Paul's blood. Had him naked on the front seat lapping up his blood. I told you."

"Sordid details aren't always necessary to make a point, Winston," Mother says, forcing gentility back into her speech.

"I am having some trouble grasping all the implications of this, Andrew," Father says, waving wife and elder son to silence.

"I know the implications," Winston says, undeterred. "Wooden stakes and mallets at sunrise ... And I become sole beneficiary." His eyes brighten as his legal mind kicks into gear. "He's dead. I'm your only living offspring," he says to our dumbfounded parents.

"I'm not cutting Andrew out of my will on that flimsy technicality," Father retorts.

Winston is taken aback. "But he died before you."

Father glowers at him. "Winny, sit down, shut up, and let me think this through before I send you to your room."

Winston obeys.

"What are we to do?" Mother asks Father. "This isn't like the other thing. We can't blame it on your spinster aunt."

I know all too well what *the other thing is;* I was never certain about my Aunt Demelza. No wonder she and I get along so famously — or infamously, from Mother's point of view.

"Estelle, I don't think searching for someone to blame is in order," Father replies. He turns to me. "You didn't choose to die and become a what — a vampire — did you, Andrew?"

"I was chosen. Picked out of the crowd, you might say."

"Hardly as damning as *the other thing.*" Father winks at me. "You have nothing to be embarrassed about, Estelle. It's just one of those things." Father consults his watch. "Giles and Victoria and Paul will be here any minute." I believe that as far as Father is concerned, the subject has been buried.

"Are we just going to sit down to drinks and dinner when he—" Winston jabs that irritating finger in my direction again, "—came close to drinking Paul dry last night?"

"There's the doorbell." Mother rises, straightening her skirt. "Promise your brother you'll behave, Andy."

"I promise," I reply.

"We're coming, Howell," Mother says to the butler's knock at the library door. Linking her arm in Father's, she whisks from the room. Winny, a cool eye on me, retreats after them.

Personally, I am as perplexed as brother Winston. My parents are Democrats, but even I wonder if they aren't taking liberalism a step further than it has ever stepped before.

❏

Winny's fiancée, Veronica, has arrived with Uncle Giles, Aunt Victoria, and Cousin Paul. Veronica ogles me. Winny drags her aside, and my keen hearing picks up: "Keep away from him. He's a killer." Veronica's lecherous laughter fills the foyer.

While the rest file into the drawing room for aperitifs, Paul latches onto my jacket tail to detain me. The teeth wounds on his throat have closed neatly to two rusty freckles. His color is better than when last I saw him. In a day or two, his veins will be as full as ever, and his straining heart will have forgotten that it was pumping less than a full load.

Paul corners me against the staircase, his fingers traipsing up and down my shirtfront. A lustful gleam fills his brown eyes.

"I knew there was something special about you," he whispers. "I suspect I'm lucky to be standing here tonight."

Not necessarily. I didn't have my switchblade with me. He could still be standing here; he would just be a colder hunk of flesh than he is now.

"Are you going home soon," he asks, "or do we have time for..." He presses his full rigid, muscled length against me.

"Sooner than that," I say. I'm making a reservation for the next flight to the West Coast. Not that I don't trust my own brother, I just think risking another day in the cedar chest might be asking for a stake between the ribs. Winny was a bit too keen on that single-heir idea to suit me.

"I'll come visit you," Paul says. His hands conform to the curves of my slacks. "I feel ... well, you know, Andrew."

Yes, I know, inseparable. That happens when a vampire allows his victim to live — a first for me. Said victim is your, quote-unquote, slave until he dies a natural death and rises as a vampire himself. My hands climb around Paul's terrain. Maybe in a few years, I'll come back and finish this before the nasty tricks of time play too much havoc on his handsome face.

In the meantime, Paul and I might have to skip drinks and dinner. I can book a later flight and still be home before the sun rises on the Pacific.

Cheriton
Peter Robins

I was glad when the guide announced briskly that we'd only glance at the Morning Room and then have tea in the gardens. Stairs have become increasingly tiresome at my age and though I'd no wish to join those, ten years my junior, who were content to gossip in the coach until it was time for sandwiches and buns, I'd found the tour a little exhausting. I was happy then to lean unobtrusively against the lintel and admire the dove gray paintwork, the lilac damask paneling, and the early Laura Knights which gave the north-facing room a mood of airy cheerfulness.

There was no restraint at the tea tables in the walled garden beyond the conservatory. For most of the old biddies it seemed a re-enactment of school treats or the street parties with which they'd celebrated George and May Teck's coronation (and that's going back sixty-five years). Most of them would have been pinafored tots. I would have been fifteen, though only just, because I'd used the cutthroat razor Dad bought on my birthday for the first time.

"...and now, boys and girls, yes, of course, you're still boys and girls, Mrs. Moss, you've all had a chance to admire this lovely wee garden. Do you know there are two dozen varieties of clematis here alone, and those Russell lupins are still looking perfect against the French marigolds, aren't they? Now can anyone guess the special name the Colonel and Countess gave to their favorite retreat?"

Few paused in their munching or in the surreptitious palming of chocolate cakes that would be smuggled back to dank bedsitters. One old dear did hazard "The Morning Garden" but that was not quite right. I was certainly not going to volunteer. Yet again, I felt one pace apart from this group. Not snobbishly. I hadn't fallen on hard times, merely different times that compelled me to take what outings I could manage with folk who prattled endlessly about grandchildren or the way their mailman was switching the gold tops for silver.

Being what people today call gay and what we referred to as "different," I felt alien to their interests and was content, at the lunch club hops in Clapham, to let them suppose I had been jilted in the Great War and, so, never married. Attempts to liberalize septuagenarians seemed a daunting prospect for too slim a reward.

"...now, what about you, Mr. ... I'm sorry, I don't know your name...?"

"That's Mr. Hodges, he'll know, he was a country lad," Annie Moss clacked between slack dentures and a rock bun.

"Mr. Hodges, then. Can you think of a name for such a glorious place all planted in yellow and purple? Now there's a clue if you know your..."

"It's called the Regency Garden," I found myself saying. "Is there a drop more hot water for the tea, otherwise I'll not sleep tonight?"

"Excellent. Are you sure you weren't cheating? You didn't read up Cheriton Hall in the library yesterday?"

"No," I said, "no cheating. Call it a good guess. Aren't yellow and purple Regency colors?"

"I think you've been here on an outing before."

The helper brought hot water at that moment and I'd no need to reply. The restless guide hadn't really a second to listen anyway, for she was already organizing a stroll through the park itself for those who felt energetic enough. I did not. At eighty-one, with an unimpaired intelligence and a shrewd use of pretense, I could avoid most activities that bored me.

The woman had been right, of course. This was my second visit to Cheriton. I can't rightly recall when I first heard the name, but it must have been connected with one of the quarterly visits of my mother's eldest sister, Aunt Finlayson. If I had, as a five-year-old, any image of the place where my aunt worked as housekeeper, it would have been of a house wrapped in trees: all of them in bolls like the cherry trees in Bushey, the south Hertfordshire village — of course it's still a village to me — where my father was gardener to Professor Herkomer. In practical terms, Aunt Finlayson's visits meant half a sovereign, so it was worth cultivating the stately lady and offering artlessly to go and play on the slopes overlooking Waterford while she and my mother chatted. Sometimes I would return early; maybe it was my father's half-day and I'd meet him by the great copper door of the Professor's Folly, carrying a basket of apricots that tasted of fruit in those days, not cotton wool as they do today. Then, as I pushed open the parlor door, I'd heard the tail end of the women's conversation, sealed with a not-in-front-of-the-child sniff.

"Just look at these brave beech leaves Bessie has brought from Cheriton," my mother would be saying, but not before I'd overheard, "...so naturally, neither the boy nor the girl will ever marry."

Slowly I matched the outlines of the jigsaw. There was a park 'round Cheriton House and there must be beech trees rather than cherries. It was evidently a picture in all seasons. And there were children too. Obviously they were older than I, else how could the idea of marriage be important? And why couldn't they, with all the money to support a mansion and twelve servants supervised by Aunt Finlayson, get married? That was a question I'd not resolved by my fourteenth year. In those days it was not a question to put to one's parents. And yet, later that summer, I stumbled on a reason why the Cheriton boy at least might not wish to marry. Maybe, like me, he'd little interest in girls, and it was always possible that, again like me, he'd known a hot and bewildering romp in the August fields with a young butcher's boy. It's a laugh to think back in times like these, when there are clubs and holiday groups and gay dances, to that twilight before the Great War when any lad wondered if he was the only such person in the world, rather as we speculate today that somewhere out there intelligences such as our own roam the galaxies.

I've read books written for schoolrooms nowadays explaining that the 1914–1918 War marked the breakup of a way of life in England. Our family lived it. In August 1914 my father died, finished by tuberculosis contracted years before in the appalling between-decks conditions of Victoria's Navy. As a sixteen-year-old telegraph boy I was hardly able to provide for a widowed mother, and on New Year's Day, 1915, she married again — a clerk in the wine trade near Waterloo. One of the early commuters, he was also a lay preacher in the local Baptist chapel. In a household such as his — no books other than the Bible on Sundays, no smoking, and — strange paradox — no drinking — I had no place. Had he suspected that my bicycle did not really break down so regularly on Stanmore Common and that Vic — the butcher's boy — and I were, in fact, exploring one another well away from the pony traps and occasional passing motor, I should have been cast out pronto among the wailing and gnashing of teeth. But there was the war and, like many another, I put up my age and volunteered. Apart from my mother, there was only Aunt Finlayson to whom I wished to say good-bye before leaving with the South Hertfordshires for France.

It was an early February morning with snow already beginning to settle between the rails as the train left Waterloo for Twickenham. Cheriton, like many business houses and family places, was by then on the telephone, and the Waterford operator, on the strength of a couple of pleasant Saturday afternoons when Vic had been unwell and Stanmore Common handy, had not charged for the call to Aunt Finlayson. The Family, as she always called the Colonel and Countess, were away, Miss Victoria having gone with her mother. Only the boy (who had to be more than twenty I reasoned) and the staff were at Cheriton. I would be welcome for lunch and might stay for tea in my aunt's room before returning on the up-train.

Aunt Finlayson's directions were clear and economical, as I might have expected. Fifteen minutes' walk through the streets hushed with heavy snow brought me to the eight-foot walls surrounding the estate. These were surmounted by iron spikes as if an invasion by Kaiser Bill was expected daily. Eventually I found the gatehouse and was let in. It must by then have been about noon, for I can recall the winter sun hanging ripe as a peach in a rough sky as I strode under naked trees to the house itself, which was sited nearer the Thames than the Richmond road.

I saw no one until I had skirted the rhododendrons which almost concealed a small summer house. Perhaps because the sunlight reflected from packed snow dazzled me, I could not see more than an outline until I was close to him. Sitting rather awkwardly I thought, on an oak bench, as though some injury to the base of his spine made the position uncomfortable, was the most handsome 22-year-old I'd ever seen. And he'd been watching, maybe appraising, me for fully five minutes. Those eyes, matching in bronze the beech leaves Aunt Finlayson had so often brought, had noticed me right enough. His looks had far more to them than the obviousness of touring actors or the withered prettiness of a curate. The bone structure was firm and the set of those eyes faunlike, a characteristic of the German race I was going to fight. That, I thought, would be from the Countess, who was Bavarian born. His skin was creamy white against silky black hair cropped short and lying uneasy. The eyebrows were delicate and the chin slightly pointed. Though he was clean shaven, I was certain that, with such a coloring, he would already be having to shave a couple of times a day. What a magnificent figure he was against the snow: something untamed, impatient with the fixed patterns and corset of society life. The black coat he wore was tailored to him like a glove. He'd turned up the fur collar against a light east wind and his coat contrasted becomingly (and he knew it) with the white lamb's wool scarf knotted in a V at his neck.

"Good morning," I called, almost certain that this must be the son and heir.

"Who are you?" He didn't take his hands from his coat pockets, hardly moved his lips, but his eyes showed an even keener attention.

"I'm Miss Finlayson's nephew. Come to say good-bye. You're Master Herne?"

"Just so. Are you staying long?"

"I'm only here for an hour or so. Lunch and a cup of tea. My train's just after six."

"A pity that. We have very few visitors. I have none."

"You'd find me very dull, Master Herne. A simple country boy."

"Not too simple, I think. I'm sure I'd find it, what's the word — sympathetic?"

"I'm not certain that I know what you mean."

I had expected that when he stood up he might limp or be ungainly as a cripple. No such thing, so I wondered if he had affected that cramped pose on the bench to show off his slim build or the firm muscularity of his legs. There was certainly no physical impediment to marriage, and I began to think I understood well enough what Master Herne meant by sympathetic company. At seventeen I was romantic as the next lad, and in those few seconds was overeager to imagine the beginnings of a companion-ship more meaningful than the careless encounters on Stanmore Common. It was then that we heard a voice shouting from the house.

"Come along, Master Herne. It's most vexing of you to hide, sir. Now come along, please, luncheon is ready."

A man of thirty-two or -three was running as nimbly as he might through a foot of snow.

"My tutor; damn the idiot."

"Tutor? Looks more like a drill sergeant to me."

Master Herne smiled and the teeth were white and quite even. Moving closer to me he spoke quietly.

"Shouldn't we meet perhaps this afternoon? To talk, of course..."

"Naturally, just to talk..." We both began to laugh, being unable to continue as the tutor was approaching.

"The summer house you passed, at four," Herne whispered close to my face as he turned toward the house. It was then I discovered he was no godling dropped in my path. His breath stank. It was a smell I remembered from the back room of Vic's butcher's shop when meat had been left accidentally over the August bank holiday. Yet this imperfection was nothing — I've discovered worse since: disloyalty, pretense; a dozen greater flaws. Anyway I was certain Aunt Finlayson would have some buttermints or cashews. Herne's breath could not mar the fantasy I was concocting; only the thought of Waterloo that night and France next day could do that. Mr. Warren, the tutor, seemed for so thickly built a man both nervous and apologetic. We walked to the house together, he constantly inquiring if Herne felt he had a headache coming on. Me, I'd seldom seen any young man as ripe with health. True, he stumbled a little — but that was knowingly — so that he might brush my shoulder or clasp my hand with what seemed a desperate tightness.

Aunt Finlayson was in the hall to meet us. With a disapproving sniff, to indicate that my uniform didn't license me to be free and easy with The Family, she took me to the servant's hall, where lunch was about to be dished up.

Though the valet had gone with the Colonel and the secretary with her Ladyship, we were still a dozen sitting down to roast chicken, two kinds of potatoes, sprouts, and parsnips with home brewed beer to wash it down.

"Make the most of that, young man," Cook said, "the last decent meal you'll be getting for many a day."

"Just like home" (well, that was what she'd hoped I'd say, wasn't it?), "everything from the garden?"

"Gittings does his best, but of course he's down to one boy now."

"The chicken home-reared too?" I asked.

It was Aunt Finlayson who answered, after running her tongue along her top lip.

"We gave up rearing fowls some time ago. Too much trouble."

"That's one way of putting it." Curtis the chauffeur was swiveling his beer glass and didn't look up.

"He looks like young Eddie." The parlor maid, Jennie, spoke for the first time.

"My nephew," Aunt Finlayson sniffed, "does not look in the least like Eddie. He favors our side of the family and we — do I have to thrape it down your throat? — are Highlanders. Eddie was a Londoner and had a cockney face."

"Jennie means he looks like Eddie did at that age, Mrs. Finlayson. Not what he looks like now."

"Oh, Curtis, how could you?" Jennie was tearing at a handkerchief.

"I'm lost," I said, jerking a drop more cream onto the pudding. "Who's Eddie?"

Aunt Finlayson pre-empted any other answer.

"Eddie was an assistant gardener here. He still does such work elsewhere, I believe. The west country, I think."

"Tell him the truth, Mrs. Finlayson. Eddie works behind hospital walls, and not on visiting days neither."

"That will do, Curtis." My aunt nodded at me. "If you've finished your trifle, we'll take our coffee in my sitting room."

It had been interesting to have met the staff I'd so long imagined, but as suddenly as they'd taken substance, they receded in importance as we talked in my aunt's quiet, orderly room. It was not likely I'd see any of them again for, if the war lasted, Aunt Finlayson would have reached retirement and moved to the cottage she'd bought near Oban. More imminent was the west front but, overshadowing all, my need to slip away to meet Herne in the summer house. It was already twenty to four. Having complimented my aunt on the lunch, I told her that I'd found it a little rich and would be glad of a handful of peppermints and a half hour to walk it off by looking 'round the grounds. As I expected, she didn't object, for I knew she wished to doze over a novel before tea. She only cautioned, "Now do be back before dark or you could lose your way. We've forty acres remember."

Of course he was waiting. I needn't have been apprehensive as I trudged through the snow that had begun to fall once more. The summer house itself was dry and Herne had brought a hip flask of brandy. We laughed and chatted and his eyes danced with the pleasure of being with me again. Now, I'd always taken the lead in any physical encounters; curiosity rather than pride, really. On this occasion, though, I found myself being explored and held in a grip so fierce that I could only guess at the loneliness and abstinence that triggered it. He would scarcely allow me to press my lips against his neck or run my fingers under his overcoat to warm them against his back.

"Why not take off your gloves? You're hot as a furnace," I murmured.

"Leave things as they are," his thumb was edging along the inside of my thigh, "my hands aren't pretty. An accident: could have happened to anyone, they tell me."

What with the cramped conditions, winter clothing, and both of us overwilling to please I knew this was not going to be the most memorable hour for either of us to look back on. Slipping another mint into Herne's mouth so that I would not need to stop my breath as he kissed me, I tried to tell him so. What could have been more delightful than his reply?

"I telephoned through to the station. You're not going to get back to London tonight, you know. The snow's thick from Richmond to Wandsworth and the trains finished ten minutes ago."

"And you didn't tell me?"

"You wanted me to?"

"So, what happens now, Herne?"

"I avoid taking the sleeping muck they force on me from time to time and you slip along to my room in the North Wing. It's the end door; say, midnight?"

"Only if you'll promise to take off your gloves. It doesn't matter, you know, when..."

He paused in lighting a cigarette. "If that wasn't just words. That it doesn't matter to you..."

"I meant it," I said and kissed the point of his left ear, noticing that there, too, a light down was spreading and he'd have to be barbered carefully in middle age. As we went our separate ways by the gate to what he called the Regency Garden, I could see little of his features in the thickening darkness. Only his eyes were luminous as he said with a desolate urgency, *"You will come?"*

Having played the charade of telephoning the station a second time, I found Aunt Finlayson pleased enough with the idea of some company over a supper tray in her sitting room. Reading each evening while the secretary was away had become irksome to her and I proved an agreeable partner for her at draughts and dominoes, since she beat me four times out of five, putting my clumsy faults down to a preoccupation with getting back to my regiment. It would have been the best part of eleven o'clock when we walked through the corridors to a small bedroom that had been made up for me.

"I'll remember this when I'm in France, Aunt Finlayson."

I'd paused by a window and was looking at the park, silent under the snow and lit by full moon. "I wouldn't welcome a night like this with the Germans only a hundred yards off."

"It's the kind of night that encourages intruders." Aunt Finlayson was tired and was determined to steer me to my room. "We find it best to lock our doors here. I think you should do the same. It's good stout pine. Sleep well now. There'll be tea and shaving water at seven."

I turned the key, waited until my aunt's purposeful steps had receded, then softly unlocked the door once more.

I'd borrowed bootblack and brushes from Curtis and some Brasso from Jennie, so I set to work smartening up my kit for the next twenty minutes. No matter what the weather in the morning, a South Hertfordshire man had to look his neatest. With boots set out under the chair on which I'd hung my tunic, I burnished my cap badge, then washed in the ewer and basin before putting on the pajamas and flannel dressing gown Curtis rustled up. They weren't a flattering fit, for I was stocky rather than tall, but I turned back the cuffs and licked my hair into shape with a dash of cold water on my comb. Perhaps in the lighting of Herne's room, a couple of pimples by my nose wouldn't be noticed, and, when the light was out — which couldn't be soon enough for me — a slight blemish would be unimportant.

Midnight, Herne had said. It was nearly seven minutes to when I checked the time by my father's turnip watch, the old faithful gunmetal I'd taken with me and which I still have. No more than a minute later, while I was practicing with a cigarette in the hope that I'd not be sick if offered one, the noise began.

A dog? If a dog then one much larger than the spaniels I'd seen Jennie feeding earlier and certainly not my aunt's comic terrier. The sound, more forceful and more frequent by the moment, came from the grounds. I went to the curtains and, easing one aside, looked out into the full moonlight crackling on settled snow. At first I detected no movement. Then there were two men stumbling, hurrying as best they might across the frozen acres. One I recognized as Mr. Warren, the burly tutor, for I'd noticed his ungainly strides earlier. Could the second be Herne himself? It was difficult to be exact for both were half-obscured by shapeless black bundles they were carrying. Sacks? No; they were nets — stout mesh that could ensnare whatever interloper it was that must very soon wake not only the household but half the locals in cottages along the road.

And then, lolloping between the beech trees away from the two pursuers, I saw it stirring up the snow in sprays as it outdistanced the runners. Since one was almost certainly Herne there was little reason to creep to his room until it had been captured. Where the beast had come from I couldn't guess, but if this was not its first appearance (and the ready nets were evidence of that) no wonder they no longer kept livestock at Cheriton.

Twenty yards ahead of its hunters, the creature headed for the house itself, bursting the elegant gate of the Regency Garden like matchwood. Two stories above I watched as it leapt again. I saw only what could have been paws, what might have been fur; heard a crash and supposed that whatever it was must have gashed itself on the windows of the Morning Room. At last I saw the faces of the two men. One, as I thought, was Warren; the other, Curtis. This meant poor Herne, waiting in his room on the other side of the house, could be sitting by an unlocked door and risking attack from some creature that had run amok.

Already I felt a protectiveness toward him. I wasn't sure that it would be welcome, for I'd heard from Aunt Finlayson that the Colonel deliberately treated his son as an invalid who was never allowed to travel or take part in outdoor pursuits, much to the open disgust of the Countess. This, however, was no normal occasion. I moved swiftly to the door. It was then that I heard the first scrabbling and panting from the far end of the corridor. A fine thing that a soldier about to protect king and country had nothing but bare hands to defend either his own relative or the friend he would soon love from an attack by some predator. Yet what else could I have done but use what strength I had to tug a mahogany chest against my door frame? As well I did so. For some purpose no rational being could fathom, the thing was at my door. Whose scent could be here but my own or the cool lavender of Aunt Finlayson?

Outside, but farther back, I could distinguish the voices of Curtis and Warren.

"Soft now; approach softly, man."

What would they do: shoot it or net it?

"Ready, Curtis?" I heard.

"Ready."

"Then ... now. Tighter at that end, Curtis; tighter."

"Careful, Mr. Warren. Your hand; now look what's happened to your hand."

"Nothing at all, Curtis. The gloves took the worst of it ... gentle with the net now. Throw the chicken. Throw it, man."

And then there was no sound but a slobbering whimper until a roar — maybe as the nets were tightened — startled me again.

"That chicken's no good and you know it. Saw for yourself in the park what's really wanted."

This morning? And my aunt had let me wander in the afternoon? Had it been loose from a cage somewhere in the grounds all day? Maybe the Countess had a sinister taste in pets.

"But that's not Eddie's old room, Curtis."

"That's as may be. I remember what Jennie said."

A moment later, Curtis again, but farther off. "That hand'll need iodine you know." The whimpering and the panting faded. Ten minutes later I walked nervously to Herne's room. At least I knew he must be safe.

For a long time no one answered, though I must have tapped a dozen times. It was Warren who opened the door, wearing only pajamas. For the first time in my life I was jealous. How did a mere tutor have access to my friend's room at that hour and so informally dressed? He appeared to be waiting for an explanation. I knew that I was owed one and stood my ground.

"I suppose that noise disturbed you," he said finally. "One of the mastiffs got loose."

"Strange mastiffs you have 'round here. Not the only thing that's strange either..."

"I don't get your drift, young man."

"I'd come to see how Herne is..."

"Master Herne is sound asleep. Never knew a thing about it. Thank you for your inquiry though."

I was not going to get past that closing door and I was furious.

"No doubt you doped him again tonight?" I lashed out.

"Maybe; maybe not. I don't think the habits of The Family are anything to you, are they? Sleep well, Mr. Hodges. Or rather, good-bye. I doubt if I'll see you again."

He was wrong there.

Next morning, Aunt Finlayson was nowhere to be seen until, as I was about to go to her room to wish her good-bye, she came downstairs dressed for the shops, although it was barely half past eight.

"I shall walk you to the station," she announced.

We were halfway along the drive before she paused in what was, for her, idle chatter that I began to think deliberate.

"Aunt Finlayson," I seized the moment, "what was going on at midnight?"

"Decent working folk were in their beds asleep, as I hope you were."

"It's not easy to sleep with some kind of creature being hunted under your window." Aunt Finlayson stopped. We had reached the rhododendrons and she rounded on me.

"I said you favored our side of the family but I was wrong. Your father was a man given to romancing. All that travel alone on the seven seas had no doubt addled his brain. A creature being hunted? We have none at Cheriton that I'm aware. No snow has fallen since last night. Where are the marks of any creature in the snow? Or have those gardeners conspired to fill them in?"

It was true. No marks.

"Now wait a moment, Aunt Finlayson..."

"I will not. I've no wish to stand here freezing while I listen to some foolish nightmare."

"Look. There were two men chasing something. Here. See for yourself: four sets of print ... or three and something that could be, well, paws."

"Probably a dog bounding after the postman. Now, let's forget this nonsense or you'll be later than you already are."

Something glinting in the sunlight under the summer house steps attracted me. I was over, had picked up three objects, and was back by Aunt Finlayson in a trice. My brain had begun to whirl.

"Where is Mr. Warren this morning?" I asked, hoping my aunt would chatter again and that I would gain time to sort the questions I really wished to put.

"Giving a lesson to Master Herne, I would imagine."

"I think you're wrong, Aunt Finlayson." By this time we were turning into the London road near the station. I had spotted Herne's tutor come out of a chemist. We chatted with him and then I said viciously, "I suppose you've been fetching some more dope for Herne. He chucked the last lot under the summer house, you know. Would you like the bottle? And he dropped his glove there as well."

I gave him Herne's right glove and the bottle with heavy tarlike remnants of tincture of cannabis. He took both in his left hand. I saluted and with a meaningless smile he thanked me. Catching him off guard I put out my hand. Automatically he pulled his bandaged right hand from his pocket.

"Sorry," I said, "last night's mastiff?"

As we hurried onto the platform, my aunt caught me by the arm.

"You know," she said, "don't you?"

"What I know adds up to less than nothing," I replied. "Tutors who look like bruisers, an assistant gardener who disappeared, and something that might have been a mastiff or maybe didn't exist at all."

"Tell me, did you like Master Herne?"

"Very much."

"So did Eddie the gardener. I called them David and Jonathan. Curtis called them something coarser, but then Curtis is a coarse-grained creature."

"And then?"

"Jennie set her cap at Eddie and she's a forward lassie."

"But what's all this to do with Herne and Eddie being wherever he is?"

"You're a foolish boy, but then your mother would marry a Sassernach. Eddie was badly injured, and Warren is, well, a keeper."

"A keeper?"

"Just so. Here's your train now. Come back to us. But not here." I waved until the bridge obscured her and then sat bewildered, hurt, and, yes, frightened. I needed a cigarette. Instead of the Woodbine packet, my fingers closed on Herne's left glove. I smoothed out the cream velour wondering if I might ever see him again and then put it in my tunic pocket with the turnip watch. It must have been all of two years later in an army field hospital that I actually tried on that glove, recalling Herne and Cheriton. When I withdrew my hand there were half a dozen strong black hairs — not my own — adhering to my wrist.

"Mr. Hodges. I do declare, Mr. Hodges, you've been having forty winks. Come along now, the coach is ready by the summer house."

As the guide strolled with me I asked what had become of the family. It had, she explained, died out during the Great War. The Countess accidentally shot her son one winter's evening. The Colonel then became a recluse and died of a heart attack on Armistice Night. The daughter never married.

As we reached the coach I suggested, "That accident with the gun. Would it have been in February perhaps, at full moon?"

"Now I know you've been in the area before," laughed the guide, "that's the kind of story scatty Jennie at the sweet shop invents. Lot of old nonsense."

The Succubus
Jess Wells

She timed her arrival to the corner well: without breaking her stride, Margarite stepped into the bus as the last passenger entered, dropped in exact change, and slid into a seat alone.

There should be no reason for feeling flustered, she thought, a bit confused. Her clothes were clean and well pressed, her hair combed in place. Even her briefcase was tidy, and she was well prepared for the meeting she had called.

I'm not really flustered, she puzzled, but something felt amiss, remnants of a bad dream that delays my breakfast, makes me forget where I've put the jam, or something. Silly, really. Margarite smoothed the collar of her tucked white shirt and its thin black bow.

There was ... it was ... wait, her forearm told her, it was her breast. There was a burning, in her breast, like a mouth on her nipple and (she shifted in her seat) now a pinching feeling, was it ... teeth on her nipple? No, of course not. Margarite looked down at her blouse, then glanced to the side (was anyone looking?). Could anyone see her hardening nipple and she swore there was a tongue running 'round and 'round its crumpled skin.

Margarite cleared her throat, straightened the crease in her slacks, and pulled her briefcase in front of her. Absurd, she thought, the flush growing in her cheeks, I'm on the 8 Market toward Sansome Street, just like every morning.

But she swore there was a mouth on her breast, circling her nipple, taking bites.

The bus lurched to a stop and Margarite braced herself with a hand on the seat in front, left it there to shield the excited breast. Maybe if she read the paper, she thought, but she didn't want to take her hand down. A woman with a large parcel edged past her seat, a young girl in tow. Businessmen, oblivious to everyone, pushed down the aisle. People were standing up now, holding the railings, their bellies at eye level, so Margarite stared straight ahead. She couldn't move, pressed against the seat by the busy lips inside her blouse. Her breathing deepened. She was pinned, trapped by the suck, suck, bite.

I am *not* a prisoner, she thought, I am Margarite Le-Carr, I am going to work like any morning. I slept alone last night, in pajamas, and I do *not* have ... lips on my nipples. The idea was absurd; never mind the feeling, the thought of it was preposterous. I'll read some papers for the meeting — mind over matter, she thought, and set down the briefcase between her legs and yanked out a folder. Ah, she could move from the back of the seat. Margarite smiled. It must have just been ... my bloods or something.

But the woman didn't get the folder opened before the tongue flattened and covered her entire breast with wetness, wiggling a tongue point into the crease between breast and chest. Margarite gasped, looked sideways. Her breast was being lifted up, sucked. She could feel the spittle running down her mound onto her belly. She could see it, she could, the surface of her left breast higher than the right, being held and now kneaded and squeezed. Margarite cleared her throat and pulled up her collar.

"Excuse me," Margarite said, as she gathered her things to her chest and scurried out of her seat. The man beside her looked puzzled. Margarite pushed through the crowd, gasping and whining as her nipple was twisted. "Pardon ... me ... ah ... oh, excuse ... Aah, coming through ... *back door!*"

❏

"Good morning, Mr. Taylor," she said as she stepped into the wood-and-chrome elevator.

"Good morning, Ms. LeCarr."

"Margarite."

"Tom. Hello, Harold," Margarite tried to steady herself. She turned. "Vivian, good morning, dear."

Up the floors and out the doors, the workers held their attaché cases and their styrofoam coffee, raincoats over their arms, a higher class of knit suits remaining as the numbers climbed.

In her office, Margarite set her briefcase down as if the journey had taken months. What was going on with her body? At forty-three her hair was graying and crow's feet cut in toward her deep-set eyes. She had a round belly and wide thighs, long fingers, a regal carriage. But this morning she felt like a girl, confused by her first blood.

Margarite poured herself coffee. Diane, her assistant, was already in: the phones were on hold and Margarite could hear the file drawers rolling back and forth. She ran her finger across her manila files but wandered aimlessly into the front office.

"Good morning, dear," she said softly.

"Good morning, Marge," Diane said with a grin, spunky, looking up from the folders to study the woman's face. Diane was thirty-five, with hair as thick as a dog's and a nose that drew a viewer up its arching smoothness to her eyes. Constantly moving, Diane always looked like she'd just gotten off the racket-ball court, no matter what she wore. There was always the telltale pink in her cheeks.

The two women knew each other's lines and wrinkles, they knew what puffy eyes in the morning meant. Diane had listened to many stories of Karen leaving Margarite and moving east and she had been gentle during those months of pain when Margarite stared out of the windows and cried during lunch.

"I forgot our breakfast," Margarite said softly, "I'm sorry, falling down on my job."

"Well, those blintzes are a hard act to follow," Diane said, flashing brown eyes and giving her friend an out. When Margarite didn't take the bait, Diane scanned her face closer. "Bad dreams?"

"No," Margarite said hesitantly, averting her eyes. She wasn't sure what was happening. How could she explain this, even to Diane, her only confidante?

"Well," Diane said, shoving the file drawer closed, "no time for breakfast anyway, only twenty minutes before this fucking meeting."

"Right," Margarite said, and returned to her office, where she opened her curtains to the sun and plopped into her high-backed chair. Her coffee sat steaming on the file cabinet in the other room while she stared out at the willow trees, their tendrils languorously streaming in the breeze. They dipped and skittered across the morning.

This was not her imagination, she reasoned. And nothing unusual had happened to precipitate it. The night before she had not dreamed, she had not touched herself or slept naked. She had lain motionless — perfectly smooth and tucked sheets told her — for eight hours and thirty minutes, the same celibate night she had lived for the nine months since Karen had left her for a new job and a new woman on the East Coast. Her body was something that sat behind her desk, sat at a café table, lay cold under sheets at night. It was better this way, easier.

Sex wasn't even something she thought about, except occasionally when she was in a crowd of lesbians and she found herself imagining things — her hand against a woman's cheek while she stood talking about business, or the shape of the breasts on a woman across the room, or her hand slipping across the small of a woman's back, embracing, touching, kissing anyone in range. It happened rarely. She was just more controlled than that.

But this ... this attention, well it was wrong, it was bizarre. Next time she would have to be sure it didn't show. Margarite turned her chair from the window. Next time? she asked herself, you're planning on it? Margarite remembered the feeling of her breast being lifted up and a flush rose through her body.

Now, what was this feeling ... no, not again, she thought and smoothed the front of her blouse. No, it was not her breasts, but there was a tingling ... in her legs. Margarite sat back in her chair. Like the touch of a feather tipped with down, the sensation ran up her ankles to her calves and played behind her knees, bringing her blood up inch by inch. Suddenly, it teased the curve of her hipbone and drew across the top of her thigh. Her mouth opened and her eyes glazed over. It stroked the side of her neck; she laid her head back and gave her temples to it. To what, she thought, to whom?

It brushed her lip; she shivered and turned away; the feather proceeded and the willows outside draped themselves through the air like a dozen soft boas. The feather took her back and forth, rhythmically, in long sweeps up the front of her body, then down her shoulders and across her buttocks, as if she were not sitting, as if she were not clothed, not on the twelfth floor with things to do.

Margarite swayed in her chair, eyes closed, the muscles of her neck standing out, red from ears to chin, little beads of sweat gathering under her nostrils. She allowed herself to be lulled into the rhythm.

Just then, her tormentor switched from feather's down to quill tip, and dug into her shoulder. The pain burned her skin. Diane walked into the room with Margarite's coffee cup. The quill scraped from shoulder to base of the spine.

"Margarite, you left your..."

Margarite shuddered. As she grimaced, the phantom plunged fingers into her cunt, up where it was wet from her bus ride. The pain drained hot from her shoulder to her vulva, giving her a bigger hole and a throb like a drum. She slammed her hands on the table.

"Ahh, I'm not well," Margarite stammered, "I mean I..." She watched Diane take inventory of her flushed face and unfocused eyes. Oh, not *here*, Margarite pleaded silently. What am I saying? Not anywhere, leave me alone.

"I need to go home," she said, pleading.

"Home? You? But the meeting!" Diane replied, confused, shocked. "Home?"

"Oh, yes. Well ... you can handle it. Yes," Margarite said, brightening. "That will be fine. We've been over the proposals a number of times, Diane. You helped write them. It's a fine opportunity for the board to see..."

"Margarite," Diane said, warning.

"...to see how valuable you are. How capable. It's a wonderful idea," she said, standing up and searching for her papers. "Really, Diane, this can't be helped," she said, not quite certain what she meant.

"Is it your stomach?" Diane asked.

"No."

"The flu? Your joints feel all right? Margarite, you're a wreck. You don't look sick, you look absolutely frazzled."

The two women stood silently while Margarite packed her briefcase, hoping it at least resembled the papers she brought in this morning, trying to lay out the proper folders for the meeting. The stalemate continued, a tight silence in the office, until Margarite picked up her report and handed it across the desk.

"Here, you'll need this."

"Oh, god." Diane paced the width of the room, exasperated. "All right ... I'll call you a cab."

Margarite sat back in the taxi, her beige linen coat draping on the seat, her legs crossed at the ankles. The cap plunged up Market Street, the reverse of the route she had just taken. This is the first time that I have ever, she thought, taken a day off work for ... nothing ... for sex. Margarite was incredulous. In how many years of being sexual, she thought, and why now? And how could she be expecting to ... and so didn't that mean that she was an accomplice and so making love with ... this ... phantom, this ... succubus?

Yes, that's what it is, a succubus, a woman spirit who comes to seduce in a woman's sleep. She had read about them in reference to the saints. A nun locked in a convent ·cell and denied the world, except a view of the herb garden from her barred window, would be visited at night by the spirits of women.

The succubus came when the nun had spent the day watching the bent backs of the novices in the fields, torn by the sight of women so far away, as her pen and ink and scriptures sat idle. The nun would go to bed early, slipping under her coarse cotton sheet, still in her hair shirt. She would toss and turn. A touch would come to her, her temperature rise. "No, no, I mustn't," she would murmur but turn her buttocks to the moon. The succubus would laugh and, hovering above the length of her body, set her mouth on the nun's ass.

In the morning, the nun, her eyes sunken from the lack of sleep, her hair wild, would be found in the corner of her cell by the novices who brought her breakfast. Gripping the windowsill, her neck covered with black-and-blue bites, black-and-blue shoulders and forearms, the nun would grit her teeth against her words and the novices, prohibited from stepping inside the threshold, would stare open-mouthed at the woman's bare legs and cold toes.

"Sister Angelina! Do you ... require anything?"

The taxi that took Margarite home pulled smoothly into the drive. She sat very still in the back.

"'Scuse me?"

"Yes? ... oh, of course, how much do I ... Oh, I see, $4.50." Margarite fumbled in her briefcase. "Keep the change." She leaned forward with the money and caught a glimpse of herself in the rearview mirror, her neck purple with bites. She dropped the bill onto the front seat and pulled up her collar, her breath caught in the chest.

"Ah, Miss, it's a bit short here. That's $5.50."

"Oh. Yes. Excuse me, let me give you two. Thanks again," she said weakly and slid out of the door. She opened the collar of her coat and pulled on her clothes, seeing just what she expected — black-and-blue marks all over her shoulders. As the taxi drove away, she stood clutching her lapels. What I see, I am, she thought, and what I think, I feel. Oh, Goddess, this is very dangerous.

Margarite stood in the drive looking up at the second floor of the peach Victorian where her curtains slowly blew in and out of the open windows. It had been years since she had seen her tiny front lawn in the daylight of a working day. She opened the front door and climbed the polished stairs to her apartment. Everything was the same as she had left it: the plants at the top of the stairs, the French doors open to the front living room, pillows just so on the green velvet sofa, armchairs, fireplace, candlesticks, closed and polished writing desk — it was all the same, but so peaceful that Margarite felt she was disturbing something. She looked at the light on the polished floors, the way the flowers looked in the afternoon, everything in the room a different color than she saw in the evening. She sat her briefcase down on the sofa, hung her coat up, her short heels clacking on the floor. She turned back to her living room. She felt like an intruder.

Margarite moved to the china cabinet by the fireplace and lifted down a tumbler, opened another cabinet for the Scotch, and strode into the kitchen for ice.

Back in the living room, Margarite kicked off her shoes and plopped into an armchair, set her feet on a square footrest. I guess I must work like my mother, she thought. Four years without a single break.

Her mother would come home tired and disgruntled and ease herself into her overstuffed chair with lace doilies on the arms. Mrs. LeCarr would fold her coat over the arm, pry her shoes off with her stockinged toes, and sigh.

"Gite, baby," she cooed to the young Margarite, waiting by the television, "come rub Mother's feet, please, baby, I work so hard."

Margarite would turn on the television and hurry to pull up the ottoman. This was the finest part of the day. Mother worked sooo hard, she deserved attention, and Margarite was happy to give it to her. The little girl scanned the TV guide every afternoon: what would Mother like? She prepared the woman's special chair, polished her table. And when Mrs. LeCarr finally came home, the little girl would hold back, expectantly, waiting for her favorite phrase: "Gite, baby, come rub Momma's feet, please, baby." Flushed and silent, Margarite would hurry across the room, sit on the flowered ottoman at the woman's side, and grasp one of her ankles. She would knead and rub and hold the foot like a breakable object, like a lamp to rub to make wishes come true.

"Momma?"

"Yes, pet," the woman sighed, stroking her daughter's head but never moving her eyes from the set.

"I can't do a good job through these stockings."

"What, dear? Oh, well, all right. You can take them off, Gite." The two had a special ritual. Mrs. LeCarr would remain totally still as Gite slid her little hand under the tight A-line skirt to her garter belt. Or the woman would slowly pull her skirt up to expose the clasp, one side at a time. The little girl's eyes took in every inch. Gite was so gentle, the soft warm thigh making her hands tingle. She grasped the black garter with both hands. Gite's body was hot everywhere, her nose overcome with the smell of her mother. She slid the sheer stocking down the thighs, dragging her little fingers along the flesh, over the knee, across the calf and off. Gite let it accordion-fold onto the floor. Mrs. LeCarr leaned on her other buttock to receive her daughter on the other side.

Now, with her hands on flesh, Gite would massage with a new vigor, rolling the soft skin between her thumb and finger, stroking the calves, pushing into the arches, pouring all the energy, the expectation of the afternoon, into her mother's skin. "I work so hard," her mother would say, "I deserve my..." whatever it was at the time: her Sunday sleep, her fancy food. Work made it right, and for Gite, hard work made this skin and touch and caress, made these woman smells possible; hard work meant Gite's hand slipping into the tight, hot space between the hem and the panty leg.

Today, in her own apartment, forty-three and ill at ease, Margarite sat forward in her seat. You do *not* fantasize about your mother, she thought. Margarite glanced at the bruises on her shoulders and, setting her Scotch glass on her knee, felt her shoulder blades for the beginning of the scratch. You've never touched your mother above the knees and you better not start thinking about it now, goddamn it. Margarite leaned her head against the chair back and closed her eyes.

"Momma, I can't do a good job through these panties," she murmured. 'All right dear, you can take them off.' Let me sit between your legs, you work so hard, let me nuzzle inside your folds, let me bite your thighs, Momma. I want to see your head against your chair, I want spit sitting in the creases of your lips, give me your titties again, different this time. My mouth on your cunt, my lips teasing your lips, fingers pulling your hair, Mother, spread your legs further, that's right, touch my ears with your thighs, I'm eating you. Yes, yes, drape me back across the ottoman, my pigtails on the rug, I know the tops of these thighs, Mother, to slip my hand around the back to your buttocks, one hand in back, one hand in front, a little girl wiggling into your cunt, I dive again, my fingers plunging in while I eat you, Mother, my little girl's fist sucked back up where it belongs, fucking you, Mother, you scream for *me* at night.

Margarite opened her eyes. Wide. She was ... good Goddess, she breathed, she was draped backwards across the ottoman, the afternoon sun striping her belly and legs in her executive clothes. The Scotch glass was spilled on the floor. The smell of a woman was heavy in the air. Margarite clambered up off the floor with difficulty. Her hand ... was wet. Viscous come clung to the webs of her fingers, curled into a fist.

It can't be, she thought, turning in a circle, scanning the room for a woman she knew she wouldn't find. The succubus was in control, could make her fantasies more real than she had ever wanted. Tears welled up in Margarite's eyes. I do not cry, she thought, but look at me. She turned to the mirror. I don't have sex, but I've been fucked on a bus, in a cab, in my office. I'm covered with bites and bruises and scratches and, she eyed her hand with suspicion, I fuck. She wasn't really in control anymore. She knew that now. Even though she felt she was totally in charge of herself, her cunt had always broadcast her need to her constantly, feeling so swollen and insistent it was as if it walked a few inches in front of her. Now Margarite knew that she had never been in control of her body — she had consistently denied its needs but had never controlled its desires and now the succubus had taken away even her ability to deny herself. She was being fucked and, she smelled her hand, she was fucking. Truly now, she was what she thought and she felt what she saw.

Joe Louis Was a Heck of a Fighter
Jewelle Gomez

Gilda is more than alive. The 150 years she carries are flung casually around her shoulders, an intricately knit shawl handed down from previous generations, but distinctly her own. Her legs are smooth and mocha brown, unscarred by the knife-edged years spent on the Mississippi plantation and strengthened by the more-recent nights dancing in speakeasies and discos. The dichotomy did not escape Gilda. Her power was forged by deprivation and decadence and the preternatural endurance that had been thrust upon her. Her grip could snap bone or metal and when she ran she was the wind — invisible and alone.

Tonight, going home to Effie, she walked easily, gazing at the evening skyline. The tree-shrouded park sloped gently downward from the city street to the sluggish river. The soft flowing of the Hudson played in her ears, obscuring the city sound, evoking the other rivers by which she's lived — the Mississippi, the Missouri, the Charles. Through the years she'd made many towns her home and in that time found much to remember fondly. In spite of the unease caused by the proximity of the running water, Gilda often chose the river as a place of comfort. Its movement helped her believe in the endurance of all life, not just her own. It also reminded her of her own vulnerabilities. She looked out into the darkness and the river sparkling under the moon and smiled. It had been a good life, one full of newfound family, explored places, and action. She felt herself a part of more movements and change than she'd believed possible.

Whenever she thought perhaps it was time for her to consider the ending of this long life she remembered how much more was left to be done. And she thought of Effie. They'd spent much of the past few years together seeing what the world offered, seeing what they with their special powers might offer the world. Effie's presence had changed almost everything about Gilda's life. Even her memories took on more resonance. She was able to learn from her past in a way she'd not known she could. The life they led, its possibilities, seemed fruitful, not simply endless. She'd not noticed before how important hope was to living.

Gilda realized she'd stopped and turned from the river to listen to the trees. Ahead of her through darkness Gilda saw a man leaning against the park fence, hidden from the streetlight by the shadows of a thick maple. Her body tensed but felt no fear. He was in his twenties, strongly built, and obviously up to no good. But he was only a man, while she ... well, she knew the ropes. She pushed through the darkness to probe his mind. There, she was swept up in his swirling confusion and singed by his rage. The core of his thoughts was painfully unfocused but his immediate intent was unmistakably directed at her.

Gilda felt the anger well up inside of her, something she'd only recently learned could be helpful. She did not push it down inside but let it wash over her as if it were the flowing river with an irresistible current. Her mother, Fulani, features hemmed into a placid gaze, had not been allowed that luxury. She'd been a slave, admonished to be grateful, not angry. As a child Gilda had not understood: the master who owned all and was responsible for everyone never showed anger. His wife, whom he pampered and worshipped oppressively, was angry all the time, as was the overseer, who regularly vented his anger on black flesh. But they were not thought to have anger any more than a mule or a tree cut down for kindling.

Gilda remembered that first time the anger had caught her unawares. Alone on the road, more than a hundred years before, two white men first thought she was a boy. They approached on their horses with only their leers lighting the night. When they realized she was a woman, their attentions felt much like this young man lurking ahead of her. They'd swung down from their saddles easily, as if the encounter had been prearranged. For a moment Gilda had forgotten her powers and shown simply the fear of a young girl, which enticed them even more. They spoke of teaching her a lesson — one man raising a whip in his hand, the other fumbling with his belt. It was the pressure of his hand on her shoulder that sent the shock of anger through her body. She'd struck upward at his face with a blind power that she didn't know she possessed. The clumsy blow snapped his head backward, breaking his neck. He crumpled at her feet before she realized she'd even hit him.

The other man stood frozen, disbelieving. Only when Gilda snatched the whip from his hand did he know that he too was in danger. He moved backward gingerly, then turned and ran toward the brush. Gilda snapped the whip above her head, laying it out through the air above his head. She moved quickly toward him and laid open his back with the next stroke. He'd fallen facedown in the dirt and had begun groveling away from her. She snapped the whip one more time, across his legs, and watched the blood well up through his pants. He tried to stand but soon fainted from the pain and shock.

She'd turned away quaking with the anger, sickened by the result of her unchecked power. It was another reminder of how alone she could be. She returned to the man who lay dead and turned him over so his pale face shone in the moon light. Without its wicked grin it looked much like a boy's. She'd gazed intently at the features as she'd been taught to do, taking in the look of him, the feel of him, and who he'd been. His face and the sense of his life were stored in a private place deep inside, always to be remembered. As the taker of his life, this was her duty. Gilda seldom returned to those memories, those faces, and did not want to add to their store.

The young black man stood under the maple, his intentions leering out from behind an empty grin. The thought of those faces deep inside almost made her double over in pain. The boy ahead was so many others she'd known in her life: on the plantation scratching at life, on the streets of this city celebrating life. She tried to make these connections so the anger didn't overtake her. She maintained her pace and continued in his direction, hoping he was simply about to ask directions or for a match.

As she walked past he spoke low, almost directly in her ear. "Hey, mama, don't walk so fast." Gilda continued on, hoping he would take his loss and shut up. He didn't. "Aw, mama, come on, be nice to me." The anger speared her, leaving a metallic taste in her mouth. Where were the words for what she felt? Gilda stopped and turned to him, smiling as she remembered the words of an irate Chicago waitress in 1962: "I am not your mama. If I were I would have drowned you at birth."

She walked on. Sprinting lightly he caught up with her. She could smell the spicy scent of his after-shave lotion and caught the glint of his jewelry. "Why you bitches so hard? Come on, sistuh, give me a break!" The insistence in his voice was almost reasonable, as if he actually believed she might want to stop and be with him. She walked on. "Come on, little girl, let me see that smile again." With that he seized her arm in what he thought was a viselike grip.

She shook free easily, leaving him off balance. Surely he'd let go of the idea now — the idea that bruising her would somehow give him power. Gilda let the anger swirl around inside her but consciously listened to its grasping tide. It receded somewhat as she turned to look directly at him. In spite of his height he really wasn't much more than a boy. She started to speak, but the coldness that descended over his face stopped her.

Without another word he snatched at her close-cropped hair, hoping to pull her into the shadows. Rage replaced the smile on Gilda's face, and a low moan sounded in the back of her throat. She could almost see her slim fingers clenched around his neck, snapping the connection to the spine. The memory of that night long ago came rushing back at her. She knew how easily it would be done.

She replaced that vision with the memory of a hot night in Florida in 1950. She'd been sitting in an after-hours club watching the café-au-lait-skinned fighter show how he'd whipped a Tampa boy who'd said boxing was just a "coon show." His moves had been swift and delicate, the power behind the fist firmly steered by a balletlike thrust of his arm. The veins in his arms were cords of electricity. The point in the air where his fist stopped almost glowed with the energy he'd directed there.

Gilda smiled again as she raised her fist and smashed it into the man's jaw. He fell unconscious to the cracked pavement, half sprawled on the thin city grass. Gilda lifted him from the street, so that he sat against a tree, and knelt low, hiding them from the traffic. His flesh opened smoothly as she sliced behind his ear with her fingernail. She took her share of the blood swiftly, enjoying the warmth as it washed over her, exploring his mind as she held him. The rage that had welled up inside of her was matched by his. He lay as still as a sleeping child, yet inside was despair and anger which almost made his body pulsate.

Gilda took the blood, trying to push away the anger, both hers and his. But the impulse remained to stand with the limp body and hurl it through the trees into the river. Instead she pulled back inside herself — where she'd been before this encounter. The hope she'd been thinking about infused her thoughts and she spread that energy outward over the almost-emptied mind of the young man in her arms. For all blood taken something must be left behind — hope would be as good an exchange as any. Gilda wrapped his mind in hope, visions of future, a more solid sense of himself in the present. It was a small gift, and it was a relief to not add his face to that secret gallery.

Gilda took such a quantity of blood that the young man's body realized it was in danger. She could feel it struggle to maintain itself, so she pulled back, letting that desire to survive blend with its newfound hope. She looked down at the hardened face as she held her hand to seal the wound.

The sound of the river below and the trees seemed to return to conceal their thoughts. She held her hand at his neck until she could feel his faint pulse become steady. She lifted him with fluid ease. His body was limber in her arms as she lay him stretched out on a wooden planked bench that sat facing the river. She arranged his arms under his head so he looked as if he'd just laid down for a short nap. He even snored gently. In the brief time it'd taken to move him his face had softened. The tight line of anger across his brow had dissolved and the bend of his mouth was turned more upward than down.

As she rose to leave Gilda was glad she had such a good memory. "Yeah, Joe Louis was a heck of a fighter," she said aloud. Gilda turned swiftly, disappearing inside the wind blowing off the river. She was late for home and Effie.

Sacrament
Adrian Nikolas Phoenix

Silver leaned his aching body against the bridge's low concrete wall and glanced down at the black waters of the Willamette River. Bright neon reflections shimmered across its surface, and he imagined he saw the hot pink letters of ALL NUDE REVUE dance over the blackness. Maybe he had. Club 69 squatted at the right-hand end of the bridge.

Narrowing his eyes, Silver tried to gauge the distance to the water. He feared the fall wouldn't be enough. He'd heard stories of people who'd tumbled from the Golden Gate in Frisco and survived. Maimed, vegged out, but alive. And this bridge wasn't nearly as high as that one. He touched his jeans pocket, the hard lump of the pocketknife inside reassuring him. Just before he jumped, he would slit his wrists. Then if the fall didn't kill him and he didn't drown, at least he'd bleed to death.

He rubbed sweaty palms back and forth along the mist-sprayed wall, barely feeling the concrete's rough bite. His stomach knotted and he swallowed heavily. Fifteen years old and dying of AIDS. A stupid way to go, it wasn't even noble. His hero, the Silver Surfer, wouldn't have been caught this way. He would have guided his surfboard past the waves of illness and into the cosmos beyond.

Fifteen years didn't seem like a very long time, yet sometimes, like now, it felt more like forever — sucked dry, hollowed out, but still hurting.

Yeah, like fucking forever.

A breeze drifted up from the river, smelling of fish and decay. Its coolness stole some of the fire from his body. Silver closed his eyes. He wished for a place to lie down and sleep.

Tell me a bedtime story, Daddy.

Silver tried to take a deep breath, but coughed instead, and pain lanced through his chest. Weak and soaked in sweat, he sagged against the wall. Once the spasm passed, he eased onto the wall. Straddled it. Winos and transients shuffled past, paying him no mind, the collars of their long, dirty coats turned up against the late April chill. A few yards ahead stood a dark-haired man wearing a tan windbreaker. He slouched against the wall, his attention on the passing cars.

Satisfied, Silver dug the knife out of his pocket and fumbled it open. He stared at the blade, feeling sick to his stomach, wishing—

What?

That I could go home and that Dad would be like he was before Mom had tossed her things into the old, oil-spitting Dodge and driven into the sunset?

That I could be little again so that a glass of orange juice, two aspirins, and a hug would make the sickness go away? Poof, like magic?

Silver bit into his lower lip, bit until the taste of blood seeped into his mouth. *Now,* he thought, holding the knife above his left wrist. He steadied his shaking hand against his knee. *Now...*

A hand seized Silver's right wrist with numbing force. The knife tumbled from his fingers, bounced against the concrete with a sharp *ting,* then slid over the edge into the darkness below.

His throat tightened. "Damn it!" Silver swiveled and swung his other leg over the wall. Gritting his teeth, he shoved free of the bridge.

Fingers continued to crush his wrist.

Silver cried out as pain jolted through his shoulder. He slammed against the side of the bridge, its weathered surface scraping the skin beneath his shirt. As though he weighed no more than an empty bottle of Mad Dog, he was yanked back over the wall and tossed onto the sidewalk.

Dazed, Silver crawled to his knees and cradled his throbbing arm against his stomach. He looked up into intense blue eyes. He recognized the windbreaker, the dark hair. Silver was close enough now to see the gray threading both hair and neatly trimmed mustache. The man bent, grabbed Silver's upper arm, and hauled him to his feet.

Heart thudding against his ribs, Silver glanced down at his swollen, purple-marked wrist. He wanted to die, yes, but he didn't want to be murdered. He didn't know which frightened him more, the man's strength or the secrets his strength hinted at. Was he a PCP bone-crusher? A johnny-do-good? A psycho?

"How long have you been ill?" the man asked, voice low and harsh.

Silver stared at him, goose bumps popping up on his arms. How did he know? Then he remembered how he had looked in the mirror that morning. Bluish smudges beneath the eyes, the pallor of his skin. Tired. Remembered his own sour smell.

"How long?" the man repeated.

Silver shrugged, shifting his gaze to the traffic. How long? No way of telling. He'd worked the streets and alleys for the past year, selling himself to men who craved hungry boys in tight jeans. It earned him enough money for a room in a roach-infested hotel, new clothes, food, and comic books. Sometimes he earned enough to go dancing or to see a movie.

So when he woke drenched in sweat, the sheets cold and clammy, and not for the first time, he hadn't been surprised. He'd known the risks. But he'd hoped it wouldn't happen to him.

Muscles tight with anger, Silver said, "You've done your good deed for the day, so fuck off." He tried jerking free of the man's hold, but failed.

Fingers brushed through his hair. Silver froze. Even the cars seemed to slow, the red glow of their taillights stretching out like wedding streamers.

"Child of the flock, *tha sibh finn*," the man murmured. "Your hair is silver, like the *ban sidhe* — the pale folk — but your eyes are dark."

"Dyed," Silver said, mouth dry. "I dyed my hair. But that's what people call me. Silver, I mean." He closed his eyes, confused by the gentleness of the man's tone and the strangeness of his words. He wanted to lean into the warmth of the hand stroking his hair, to rub against the fingers like a cat. But part of him wanted to hit, kick, punch. To scream.

"You are alone," the man said.

The muscles in Silver's throat constricted. He nodded, not trusting his voice. Yeah, even his friends avoided him. They waved when they passed him on the streets, but their faces were scared. His buddy, Alias, had helped him though.

For when it gets bad, Silver, he'd said, handing him a bottle of pills. Silver had taken them all and had gone to bed. He had spent the next two days throwing up. So much for pills.

Tasting salt on his lips, Silver opened his eyes and touched his face. The wetness he felt there surprised him. He wiped his face dry with the back of a hand.

Crying is for babies. Crying is for wimps. Crying solves...

The man's fingers trailed the length of Silver's hair, brushed his cheek, then were gone. The hand on his arm relaxed. Silver looked at him, and something sparked within the stranger's blue eyes. Something that coiled, burning, around Silver's spine.

"I am Cian," the man said. Chieftain of clan Blood. If you want death, child, I can give it to you without pain." He smiled and his lips pulled back from his teeth.

Silver stared at his teeth, especially the long, slender canines. Too long. Too slender. Curved. Too real to have been bought at Woolworth's. Static filled Silver's ears as though he'd tuned between stations.

A vampire in Portland.

Why not? Silver thought. On the streets, anything was possible. Anything at all. From handing over ten percent of his nightly earnings to a couple of cops so they wouldn't bust him to free health clinics for the pets of bums and other street-folk to winos lying bloated and buzzing with flies on the sidewalks.

Anything.

An old man stumbled along the sidewalk, reeking of cheap wine and day-old shit. He stopped beside Silver. His lips twitched into a smile, revealing empty gums. "Hey, pretty," he said. "I can do you real fine. Got no teeth. Only five bucks."

Silver glanced away, nauseated. "No," he said. "No money."

Muttering about punk kids, the old man wandered away. Silver listened to the scrape of his shoes against the pavement.

Yeah, anything is possible here. Anything at all. Anything but life.

"So ... you're a vampire," Silver said after a moment. "Like in undead? Like in beware of the cross?"

Cian smiled, but this time it was a tight, closed-lip smile. "Vampire is a flock term, *gille finn.* We are the clan. And no, we are not undead."

The hand around Silver's arm tugged, and he stumbled forward. Cian's arms wrapped about him, pulling him into an embrace of heat, hardness, and the faint scent of cinnamon. Cian lifted Silver's hand to his throat. The slow, steady rhythm of Cian's heart pulsed beneath his fingertips. His own heart pounding rapidly, Silver stared at the thick, open-ended twist of gold looped around Cian's neck.

That can't be real. It'd be worth a fucking fortune.

"Forget everything you have read about us or seen on the television," Cian whispered, voice intense. "Forget garlic, coffins, and crosses. Especially the cross. You of the flock lack true understanding of it."

Silver's muscles knotted, and he lowered his hand to his side. "The *flock*, huh? Like in sheep?"

Cian shook his head. "Child, I am both hunter and shepherd."

"Make a meal outta someone else," Silver yelled, face hot. "Don't do me any favors!" He shoved hard against Cian, then winced as pain shot from his wrist to his shoulder. "Damn—" his words ended in a lung-cramping cough. His throat clenched shut. Struggling for air, he doubled over.

Steel-muscled arms spun Silver around. A fist hammered between his shoulder blades. But he continued to choke on the phlegm his lungs spat up. Static buzzed in his ears.

Don't need a river to drown, he thought, vision graying. Then the sidewalk yawned open beneath his feet and swallowed him.

❏

Silver awoke to the rumble of traffic, but the sound of it was wrong. It echoed. He breathed in the odor of mud and dead green things, his chest aching so badly he wondered if Dad had broken a rib this time. He realized he was being held, cradled like a baby. *But Dad wouldn't...*

Then he remembered the bridge.

Opening his eyes, Silver struggled to sit up, but a hand pushed gently against his chest.

"Lie still, *gille.*"

Anger flared, hot and blinding. Slapping aside Cian's hands, Silver tumbled free of the loose embrace. Pain stabbed his lungs. He knelt, then sat back on his heels, fighting the urge to cough. Mud oozed beneath his knees, cold and wet even through his jeans.

Silver stared straight ahead. He tried to think of anything but the tickling sensation deep in his chest. The river flowed a few yards away, its sluggish waters slapping against the shore. The moon's pale reflection smudged the water. *Another silver surfer,* he thought with a sudden pang. Glancing up, Sliver saw the dark curve of the bridge.

"Why are we under the bridge?" he asked. Cian didn't answer and Silver shivered, suddenly cold despite fever. He swiveled to face the man — *vampire.* "Damn you!" he yelled. "My choice. My goddamned choice! You've got no right to take it from me."

Cian looked at him from where he sat crossed-legged in the grass. His blue gaze was steady and, Silver thought, tired. "I haven't taken anything from you. Death is your choice."

"But not like this," Silver said, hugging himself. "I wanted ... I thought..." The words withered in his throat. *Thought what? That by killing myself I would be doing the brave and noble thing — that the Dark Knight, the Silver Surfer, and the Green Lantern would gather in some dark alley and speak of me in hushed tones. Nodding their heads and gazing at the stars.*

A man of honor, the Green Lantern said.

He fought long and hard, the Silver Surfer said.

But they got him. Whirling, the Dark Knight walked from the alley, his cape billowing behind him.

Silver dropped his gaze to the ground, throat tight. Heat rushed to his cheeks. *Yeah, right. So stupid.* He knew there would be no gathering of heroes, no never-never land of play all day, of eat candy all night. No place where parents held hands, and there were no black eyes or broken ribs or shattered hearts. His stomach twisted. All it amounted to was jumping off a bridge like an idiot or dying alone beside a dumpster, garbage for the rats to chew on. Or ... letting a vampire in jeans and windbreaker suck him dry.

His heart hammered so hard against his ribs that he feared Cian would see it. It leaped within his chest like some demented alien trying to burst free. He drew in several slow, shallow breaths, longing to breathe more deeply but afraid to. After a few minutes, he felt calm enough to speak. "If I choose, will I become a vampire too?" *Will I be well* was the unspoken thought.

"I don't know," Cian replied, his voice dropping to a near whisper. "I haven't witnessed a birth in nearly fifty years."

Silver glanced up at him. Fifty years? Cian looked to be in his late forties. Just how *old* was he? "But I thought..." he stammered. "I mean, in the movies—"

"I told you to forget all that." Cian stood, crossed the short distance between them, and knelt before Silver. "You have a hard head, *gille*," he said. He tugged at the edge of Silver's hair. "Despite what you believe, I sense strength within you and a warrior's instinct for surviv- al — one not limited to just this plane."

Silver stared at him, trying to make sense of his words. "Does that mean yes?" he asked.

"Only the clan priests can answer that," Cian replied with a shrug. "It is still a mystery."

A horn blared overhead, instantly followed by the screech of brakes. Silver glanced at the bridge. *Must have missed each other*, he thought when he didn't hear the crunch of impact.

"And if the choice was life?" Cian asked, the intensity of his voice yanking back Silver's gaze. "What then? What would you do?"

Silver chewed on his lower lip, not sure he understood. Cold twisted his guts. "Do?" he repeated a moment later. Cian nodded, eyes glittering. Silver glanced away, mouth dry. Cian's expression had been too much like that of a wolf's he'd seen in a zoo long ago: a hungry, restless stare. Penetrating. Only this time no concrete wall separated them. Silver's muscles coiled. He focused his thoughts, searching for an answer.

What *would* he do? Emotions surged through him, too many and too entangled to name. He knew he wouldn't go home. The hurt would be too much. Closing his eyes, Silver remembered his last night at home. *Home? Bad word for something so damned empty,* he thought. *Like Mom had yanked the soul from it when she split.* His father slept sprawled on the sofa, mouth open. His worn brown belt lay like a snake on the floor beside him, the buckle's prong a single sharp fang.

Silver watched him from the kitchen. The pungent reek of rum stung his nostrils. His stomach lurched, queasy with pain and swallowed blood. He eased down along the wall to the floor, avoiding the shattered remains of the Ron Rico bottle. As pain pulsed through him, he wished he'd never snatched it from his father's hand. Wished he'd left well enough alone. He glanced at his father. Thought of digging a knife out of the drawer and crawling to the sofa. Thought of curling beside him and crying, "Daddy!" Even thought of searching out his mother and using the knife on *her*. *I can understand why you left him, Mom. But why me? Why the hell did you leave me with him?* Words echoed through Silver, words his father had spat before laying into him with fists and belt.

You make me do this, boy. You're just not happy until I've knocked the crap out of you. Damn you.

Silver's eyes flew open. His body clenched tight as a fist. He struggled for breath. Something tore loose inside and, before he could stop it, spilled from his lips and into the night. "No!" he screamed. "That's a lie! I never wanted that. Goddamn you to fucking hell, I *never* wanted *that!*"

Cian's arms wrapped about him and Silver fought the embrace. Kicking and swinging his fists wildly, he continued to scream long after he'd run out of words. He knuckled blow after blow into Cian's body. But the man's hold never loosened. Finally, coughing and gasping for breath, Silver sagged against Cian. He felt drained. Limp.

Cradled once again upon Cian's lap, Silver listened as the chieftain murmured words in a language he didn't recognize. The smooth sound of his voice soothed like a lullaby. Silver watched the sky, hoping to see the fiery streak of a falling star. The sky remained still. He blinked away sudden tears. *There are no superheroes,* he thought. *Only survivors.*

"If I had a second chance," Silver said, voice hoarse, "I'd learn to fight back. To live." He swallowed heavily. "Surviving ain't enough." Glancing up, he met Cian's gaze.

A warm smile curved Cian's lips. Intensity flared within his blue eyes, then vanished. "Well answered," he said.

Realizing how sleepy he was, Silver rested his head against Cian's chest. The slow thud of Cian's heart lulled him, and he wished he could stay within the circle of his arms forever.

Tell me a bedtime story, Daddy.

"What did you mean on the bridge?" he asked. "About the cross?"

Cian sighed and shifted, his jacket rustling beneath Silver's cheek. Again, Silver smelled cinnamon. "Ah, *gille,* so many questions. Is it so important?"

"Yes," Silver whispered. He didn't want to sleep yet. *Just a few more minutes.*

Cian's fingers trailed over Silver's throat, tickling. Heat rushed to Silver's face. Bewildered, he closed his eyes.

"All right, then," Cian murmured. "Nearly two thousand years ago, *gille* — long before my time, but during the time of my clan mother — a young man devout in the faith of his people went into the wilderness outside Judea seeking wisdom. He found it in the form of clan Manna and was reborn. He dwelt in the desert for years learning clan ways and delving into the mysteries of self and god.

"Several things became clear to him. The history of the clans was as long and violent as that of their prey. If any were to survive, the clan feuds had to stop. Control needed to be taught to clans bound by the tides of sun and moon. The flock needed to be cared for and cultivated. Compassion and control, even during the hunger of the Hunt. So in order to bridge the gap between shepherd and hunter, he gave us the Sacrament of Bonding.

"This is my blood, drink," Cian whispered. "This is my body, taste."

Silver stared at Cian, stunned.

"You know what eventually happened," Cian said. "Many of the clans refused to give up the old ways. They believed it would make them less. Weak. The flock misinterpreted everything. Between the two he was betrayed and crucified."

"But ... that can't be," Silver said, mouth dry once again. "He came back. He rose from the dead."

Cian smiled. "The near-dead, you mean. Since the spear hadn't pierced a vital organ and hadn't remained in his body, he healed himself. Regenerated. But it took three days. Once his strength returned, he left to spread the word among the clans dwelling among other nations. His teachings took root with time."

Silver stared at the river. A campfire glowed orange and yellow on the other side of the night-blackened waters. He thought of the people huddled around it to warm their bodies before sleeping. The cold, hard ground would suck it away. And more. Silver glanced away, remembering his first night in the city.

"Is he still alive?" he asked. He felt Cian shrug.

"It's been said he died two centuries ago," Cian said. "In Venezuela, perhaps Brazil." His fingers sifted through the hair at Silver's temple.

"Cian, is it always this way with you?" Silver asked through lips gone cold. "The way you've been with me, talking and all that?"

"No," Cian murmured. "No, *gille*. This is ... different."

"Why?" Silver looked at him. Something close to anguish lined the chieftain's face. Silver's chest tightened.

"I wish to be shepherd, once," he said.

"Will my blood make you sick?"

"No."

"What happens if I survive?"

"Then you will be welcomed into the clan as my son."

As his son. Silver found he could breathe again. He looked into Cian's eyes and his doubts slid away. *One chance. One last chance.* "I think I want to sleep now," he said.

"So be it," Cian said, voice husky. He leaned forward and traced a cross on Silver's forehead. "Close your eyes, *gille*."

Silver closed his eyes and tilted his head back. His body rocked with each pulse of his heart. Cian's warm breath touched his throat, a wet flick of his tongue, then a sting as teeth pierced his skin.

Within minutes, Silver drowsed. He listened to the quiet sound of Cian swallowing and wondered if being sick made his blood taste different. Dizziness whirled into him, then left. Only the cold remained. He knew he needed to do something — *anything* — to help bring about the mystery Cian had spoken of, but didn't know what. He was too tired, too comfortable to focus his thoughts. He drifted away from his numbed body. *Death is like hiding under a bed,* he thought. *Full of cold and dark and waiting.*

What is heaven like? Memory flickered, traced backward, and Silver heard himself asking the same question of his mother, his voice too low and anxious for eight years old.

It's a place where it is sunny all day and there's no bedtime, she murmured, voice husky from cigarettes. *And you can do whatever you want. Fly. Laugh. No one to tell you that you can't.*

Fly? Like Superman?

Yeah, hon, like Superman, In heaven there are no clogged drains, no whiskey. Her eyes took on the flat, distant look that told Silver she no longer saw him. His stomach knotted. He wished he could cup heaven in his hands and give it to her. Maybe then she would see him.

There are no mirrors in heaven, she said. *Nothing to reflect the bitterness of a child grown old.*

Mama? Mama, where is heaven? He curled his fingers around hers and squeezed. The distance remained in her gaze.

Why, it's just across the horizon, honey. At the end of I-5.

Silver clutched at the blackness surrounding him, trying to tug it over him like a blanket. Instead, his fingers tore through it. Light shafted over him.

SILVER.

Cian's cinnamon scent whirled about him. *And if the choice was life?* The words vibrated through Silver's chest, the voice coming from within, yet not his own. *What then?*

Then I'd live! he cried soundlessly. His gut-twisting plunge stopped. Eyes squeezed shut, he waited for pain or the nothingness of complete death. Neither occurred. He opened his eyes. He stood balanced upon a silver surfboard. Beneath him, a white-frothed green sea tumbled against the face of a rock-strewn cliff. Rain slanted across the horizon, a thin gray veil at the world's edge.

Moving carefully, Silver knelt upon the wide surfboard and ran his hands over its smooth, solid surface. He smiled. *Real,* he thought. Butterflies swirled through his stomach. *Real.*

SILVER.

The voice sounded garbled, as though the speaker were underwater. Silver glanced down at the churning waves. His scattered thoughts gathered, narrowed into one. He knew what he had to do. Silver stood. The surfboard dipped briefly but otherwise remained steady. Wind gusted cold against him. Shivering, he regarded the long drop to the sea. He clamped his lips together. All he had to do was step forward. And pray that somewhere beneath the heaving green waves Cian would catch him.

I said I'd learn to fight back. But I might need some help at the start.

He paused at the edge of the hovering board and breathed deeply. The smells of salt, rain, and wet rock filled his lungs.

SILVER, COME FORTH.

May heaven stay forever across the horizon, Silver thought, stepping forward. Pain lashed around his ankle as he did, and yanked him backward. The surfboard tilted crazily beneath him. Falling, Silver grabbed its gleaming edge with his hands. Cold sliced into his palms. Blood, warm and thick, trickled down his wrists and along his forearms. He stared, feeling more betrayed than hurt.

Silver threw a glance over his shoulder. His father stood at the cliff's edge, a long brown whip clenched in his hand. The whip stretched beyond the cliff and out... Silver looked at his ankle. Coils of worn leather were wrapped around it. The scratched buckle with its single, sharp prong bit into the skin just above his sock. Silver choked back a scream. Sweat popped out on his forehead as his blood-slickened fingers slipped. He couldn't plunge into the sea dragging his father behind him like an anchor. He would never find the surface again. Would never find Cian's mystery.

Silver hauled himself onto the surfboard and lay there, trembling with more than just cold and strain. His stomach churned. The bitter taste of bile burned the back of his throat. Swallowing heavily, he struggled against the sickness writhing within him. And lost.

I hate you, you son of a bitch, Silver screamed. He felt the cords in his neck tighten and bulge. *I hate you! Hate you!*

The coils constricted about his ankle until all feeling had fled his foot. His breath rattled in and out of his lungs. A sick heat raged through him. Tugging at the belt-whip, his father reeled him in like some big, dazed fish.

Silver clutched at the sides of the surfboard as it jerked backward. He knew that the moment he reached the cliff he would be dead. No more dreams. No more hiding under the bed. No more chances. Just dead. He stared at the dull gleam of the board, tears blurring his vision. *So much for fighting back,* he thought. *I didn't do so hot, huh?* Blood smeared the board's surface. He glanced at his hands. The bleeding had nearly stopped.

This is my blood—

From beneath the green waves Cian called to him again, but this time his voice sounded flat and desperate.

IN THE NAME OF THE SHEPHERD, SILVER, COME FORTH!

This is my blood, Silver thought, resting his forehead against cool metal. *Drink. And thanks anyway.*

The surfboard jerked backward.

You make me do this, his father said (thought? dreamed?), the words gusting against Silver like the wind. *I don't want to, but damn it, boy, you just won't be happy until I've—*

—knocked the crap out of me, I know, Silver finished for him.

If only you'd stayed little. If only you still needed bedtime stories.

But I did! I do. But you weren't listening anymore. Or telling. Silver glanced over his shoulder. The expression on his father's guilt-and-rum-ravaged face squeezed his heart. Silver looked away, his fingers white-knuckled and bent like claws at the board's edge. He'd seen that expression before — countless times. He'd seen it on his own face in the bathroom mirror beneath the purplish bruises and split lips. The expression was one of hurt, anger, and bewilderment.

And fear.

I'm the only thing he has left to punish himself with, he thought with sudden clarity. He also realized there were more ways to fight back than just fists and harsh words.

If only you hadn't crossed the horizon, his father sighed.

That was Mom. She sacrificed us both. Silver's throat ached. *For heaven. Daddy, I forgive you. Okay? I do. Please, Daddy, please read me a bedtime story.*

The belt-whip slithered away from his ankle. Without looking, Silver knew his father was no longer on the cliff. He forced his fingers loose from the surfboard and tumbled off and into the sea.

Water surged over him. His body tingled as green splashed through his veins, cooling the ache in his joints, soothing the tightness from his chest.

Sinking...

Silver became aware that he no longer hurt, that he could breathe easily ... breathe? He no longer felt sick, the rancid taste gone from his tongue. Gone with the past. Gone with his father.

Silver.

"Silver?"

Forcing his eyes open, Silver winced at the brightness that flooded them. He blinked in confusion. It was still night! Yet he saw as clearly as if it were day. Above him, traffic rumbled over the bridge. He looked at Cian. Wetness glistened on the chieftain's cheeks.

"Cian?" Silver whispered. He tried to wipe the tears from Cian's face, but his hand was too heavy.

Cian hugged him close, burying his face in Silver's hair. After several minutes, he stood, Silver cradled against his chest. The windbreaker's zipper scratched Silver's cheek, but Silver was too sleepy to care.

"To the clan, *gille.*"

As his son, Silver thought as sleep claimed him. *God, so much to learn ... to unlearn...*

He dreamed that under the dark curve of a bridge three superheroes gathered to share word of a battle won.

Manor
Karl Heinrich Ulrichs
translated by Hubert Kennedy

F 1

ar north in the Atlantic Ocean lies a solitary and forsaken group of thirty-five islands, equally distant from Scotland, Iceland, and Norway, called the Faeroe Islands. Desolate, rocky, veiled by clouds, filled with the melancholy cries of fluttering gulls, and noisy with crashing breakers, they are almost always enveloped by fog. In summer the mountain tops, 1,800 and 2,000 feet above the sea, show rough crags, gloomy ravines, primitive fir forests, and thousands of springs, which often tumble down from great heights, foaming from boulder to boulder. The coastline is deeply cut by bays and fjords; ringed by high rocks, it is almost unapproachable everywhere. The sea, which is full of reefs all around, so as here and there to form a complete barricade, is ruffled by whirlpools formed by wild currents. Only seventeen of the islands are populated. Strömö and Vaagö are separated only by a narrow channel, which can be swum, although it takes a daring swimmer to do it. Many place names recall the time when there were no churches on the Faeroe Islands and the old belief was not yet driven out, e.g., Thorshavn on the coast of Strömö, whose name itself means "island of currents."

In those days a fisherman rowed from Strömö with his fifteen-year-old son into the open sea. A storm came up, overturning the boat and throwing the son onto the reefs of Vaagö. A young boatman on Vaagö saw this. He leaped into the waves, swam between the reefs, seized the floating body, and drew it onto land. He sat with him on a rock, holding the half-stiff body on his knees and nursing him in his arms. The boy opened his eyes.

Boatman: "Who are you?"

Boy: "Har. I'm from Strömö."

He rowed him across the channel back to Strömö, taking him to Laera, his mother. Gratefully the boy embraced his rescuer around the neck as they parted. (The corpse of his father was later thrown up onto land by the waves.) The boatman, who was named Manor, was an orphan, four years older than Har.

Manor grew fond of Har and longed to see him again. In the evening, when his day's work was finished, he sometimes rowed over to Strömö or swam the lukewarm waves, now that summer had come. Har went to the coast, climbed a cliff, and waved his kerchief when he saw Manor's boat coming in the distance. Then they stayed together an hour or two. If the sea was calm they rowed out and sang sailor songs. Or, stripping themselves of their clothing, they dove into the waves and swam to the nearby sandbar, which lay opposite; the seals, sunning themselves on the sand, fled. Or they walked in the dark green forest of tall fir trees, whose rustling tops proclaimed the speech of Thor. Or they sat down under the branches of an old birch on a rock. They chatted and made plans. If a ship were to come, which was sailing in search of whales, they both wanted to go along. As they sat there on the rock, Manor would lay his arm around Har's shoulder and call him "my boy"; and the boy never felt more content than when Manor held him in that way. If it was already late when he came, then he quietly went up to the lilac bush which shaded Har's window and knocked on the pane. Har would wake up and slip out to him. He felt so happy, if he could be with Manor!

2

A Danish three-master arrived and anchored in Vaagö safe bay, looking for sailors for a two-month voyage to catch whales. Manor went aboard and the captain immediately took on the slender-grown lad, who was in the bloom of youth. Har wanted to go along as cabin boy, but Laera complained: "You are my only child! The sea swallowed up your father. Will you abandon me?" Thus Har remained, but Manor left when the ship heaved anchor.

Two months passed; it was already wintry again. Har would climb a cliff and gaze into the distance. One morning he saw the ship coming and joyously waved his kerchief. But it was stormy and the surf was up. The ship steered toward the bay of Vaagö, but could not reach it and was thrown onto the dangerous reefs of Strömö, running aground before Har's eyes. He saw how the shipwrecked men fought the waves, and he caught a glimpse of one of them gripping a plank with his powerful arm. In the next moment he was sucked under, along with the plank, into the whirlpool of the surf. Har recognized him — it was Manor!

The flood tide brought many bodies onto land. Straw was prepared on the beach and corpses were laid on it, one next to the other. Manor's body was also brought there and laid on the straw. There he lay before Har, driven up by the sea water, with wet hair, eyes closed and cold, with pale lips and colorless cheeks from which the blood had drained. His slender form was good-looking even in death. "This is the way I have to see you again, Manor!" Har cried, and threw himself sobbing across the beloved body, for a moment tasting again the bliss of an embrace.

The bodies were brought across the channel and buried the same day in the sand dunes of Vaagö.

3

In the evening Har sat in his hut, sad and silent. Laera wanted to comfort him, but he would not be comforted; he cursed the gods. He went to bed, but could not sleep. Toward midnight he fell into a half-slumber.

Then a noise awakened him. He looked up. Something was outside at the window. The branches of the lilac bush were rubbing against themselves and their dry leaves rustled. The window opened and a figure climbed inside. Aha! He knew that figure! In spite of the darkness he recognized it immediately! With slow steps it came up to him and laid itself on him in the bed. Har shivered, but he offered no resistance. It caressed his cheeks, though with a cold hand, oh! so cold, so cold! A feverish chill made him shudder. It kissed the warm, quivering boy-mouth with ice-cold lips. He felt the wet garment of the kissing figure, whose wet hair hung down onto his forehead. A feeling of dread passed through him, but it was mixed with bliss. The figure sighed. It sounded to him as if it wished to say: "Longing drives me to you! I find no rest in the grave!"

He dared not speak; he scarcely dared to breathe. The figure had already raised itself and sighed as if it wished to say: "Now I must go back." It climbed onto the windowsill and left the way it had come.

"Manor was here," said Har softly to himself.

That same night a fisherman from Strömö was out in the channel with his boat. The sea was lighted, so that gleaming drops fell from his oar. Then, shortly before midnight, he heard a strange sound. He saw something dart through the lighted waves in the direction of Strömö, something whose form he could not make out, but which had the speed of a large fish. But it was not a fish; that much he could recognize in the darkness.

The next night Manor came again, ice-cold as before, yet he stayed longer. He embraced the boy with cold arms, kissed his cheeks and mouth, and laid his head on the soft breast. Har trembled. His heart began to pound at this intimate embrace, and Manor laid his head directly over the pounding heart. His lips sought the gently heaving knob over his heart, which had been set into motion by its pounding. Then he began to suck, demandingly and thirstily, like a nursing infant at its mother's breast. After only a few moments, however, he left off, raised himself, and departed. It seemed to Har as if a sucking animal had filled itself on him.

That night, too, the fisherman was at work in the channel. At exactly the same hour as the night before the noise came again. This time it passed close by him. In the pale moonlight he was able to recognize it; it was a swimming man. He swam lying on the right side, as sailors sometimes swim, but was dressed in a shroud. The swimmer seemed not to notice him, even though he kept his face turned toward him. He swam with eyes closed. The sight was so disturbing that the fisherman pulled up his nets and rowed away.

Manor returned the following nights also. Sometimes he embraced the boy in his sleep, for now and then sleep overcame Har before Manor arrived. He awoke then in his embrace. Each time his lips sought the soft elevation over his heart. When it became day, Har saw now and again how yet another weak little drop of blood dripped from his left nipple. He wiped it away with his shirt. A drop had doubtless already flowed by itself onto his shirt. Only on a night of the full moon did Manor not come.

A dead person is often so strongly filled with longing for one or another of his loved ones left behind that he leaves his grave in the night and comes to him. For this is the old belief, that at midnight Urda gives back a brief half-life to many and then lends them strange powers from beyond the grave. It especially happens to young people, whom a bitter death has snatched away in the blossom of their years. He who returns is filled with a great need for blood and warmth at the same time. He yearns for the fresh blood of the living and, like a lover, for embraces. He also imparts great longing, however, and often produces a violent torment.

So it was here. Har tormented himself the whole day and was afflicted. With impatience, however, he waited for night and longed for the blissful thrill of the midnight embrace.

4

Twelve days passed thus.

Laera: "You are so pale and colorless. What is the matter, Har?"

He: "Nothing, Mother."

She: "You are so quiet."

He only sighed.

In the last cabin of the village there lived a wise woman, who knew all kinds of mysteries, and the worried mother went to her. The wise woman cast runic sticks.

Wise woman: "The dead are visiting him."

Laera: "The dead?"

Wise woman: "Yes, at night; and he must die of this, if an early halt is not put to the visits before it is too late."

Laera returned home in dismay.

She: "Is it true, Har, that you are receiving visits from the dead?"

He looked at the floor. "Manor was here," he said softly and sank onto her breast crying.

She: "May the gods be merciful to you!"

He: "The gods? Bah! What are the gods to do for me now? As he clung to the plank, alas! That was the time to be merciful, if they wished. But they let him sink under without mercy. Oh, how dear he was to me!"

Then she noticed the blood stains on his shirt, so she went to the village elders. They rowed across to Vaagö with the mother and son, and they took the wise woman along. To the people of Vaagö she said:

"Your graves are not closed. One body leaves his grave each night, comes across to us, and sucks himself full of the blood of this boy."

The Vaagöers: "Well, we'll fasten him."

They took a fir stake, as long as a man and thick as his arm, and hewed it on four sides with a hatchet, making a foot-long point at the end. They walked to the dunes, one carrying the stake, another a heavy ax. They opened Manor's grave. He lay there before them, peaceful and quiet in his burial shroud.

First Vaagöer: "Look! He is lying just as we laid him down."

Wise woman: "Because each time he again lays himself in the old position."

Second Vaagöer: "His face is indeed almost fresher than usual."

Wise woman: "No wonder. For that, Har's face is now all the more colorless."

Har climbed down and threw himself once more on the beloved body.

"Manor! Manor!" he cried in a voice full of anguish. "They want to impale you. Manor, wake up! Open your eyes! Your Har is calling you!"

But he did not open his eyes. He lay there motionless under Har's embrace, just as twelve days before on the straw on the beach.

Har did not want to let him loose. They tore him away and set the point of the stake on Manor's breast. Moaning, Har turned and fell on his mother's neck, hiding his face on her shoulder.

"Mother!" he cried out. "Why have you done this to me?"

He heard the flat head of the ax fall into the stake, making the stake groan. A stronger blow, again a blow, and a half dozen more.

First Vaagöer: "Now he's fastened."

Second: "Now he'll have to give up his returning."

They carried Har away, half fainting.

"Now he'll leave you in peace, my dear child!" said Laera when they were again in their hut.

He went to bed grieving. "Now he will come no more!" he said to himself sorrowfully. He was tired and faint. Disturbed and restless, however, he tossed on his bed. Slowly the minutes crept by; the hours lazily crawled past. Midnight came and still no sleep sank over his eyelids.

Listen! What is that? In the lilac bush ... But no, of course that was impossible. And yet! Again, as before, the branches of the bush rustled and the window was opened. Manor was there again. He sighed deeply. In his breast he had a huge wound, which was square and went all the way through to his back. He lay again on Har, embraced him, and sucked. He sucked more demandingly and thirstily than before.

But Laera next door woke up that night, listened, and shivered. Early in the morning she came in and went up to Har's bed.

She: "My poor child! He was here again after all."

He: "Yes, Mother. He was with me again."

The bed was indeed spotted with the corpse's blood, which had trickled from the great wound.

5

Some hours later a boat was again rowed over the channel, but without Har. They again walked to the dunes, again opened the grave. The square stake was still stuck in the tomb, but no longer in Manor's breast. He lay bent around the stake. The stake hindered his lying stretched out.

Wise woman: "He was able to get loose. The stake is the same thickness above and below."

First Vaagöer: "He was able to twist himself from below to the top of the stake."

Second: "But it must have cost him a monstrous effort."

On the advice of the wise woman they hewed that day a stronger stake, which they left twice as thick above as below, so that it looked like a nail with a head. They pulled away the old stake and drove in the new one.

"There! Now he's nailed in," said the axman, as he gave the stake's head the last blow.

Second Vaagöer: "Let him twist and turn; he'll never twist himself loose from this."

Laera returned to Har and told him what had happened. "Now it's over," she said to herself, as she went to bed. She lay there sleepless. Midnight came and still all was quiet. Nothing rustled outside at the window in the branches of the lilac bush. No swimmer frightened the fisherman anymore, such as had cut through the billows at night with closed eyes.

Laera: "Now you are at peace from him. He tormented you so!"

He: "Oh, Mother! Mother! He did not torment me!"

He pined away in vain longing. "Mother!" he said. "It's all over with me now." He wasted away, so that he was no longer able to raise himself from his bed.

She: "You are so tired and weak, my dear son!"

He: "He is drawing me down to him."

One morning she sat by his bed while he still slept. A month had gone by since the shipwreck. It was still early. She was crying. Then he opened his eyes.

"Mother," he said in a weak voice, "I must die."

She: "Oh no, my child! You should not die so young!"

He: "But yes! He was with me again. We talked with one another. We sat on the rock under the old birch in the forest as usual. He wrapped his arm again around my neck and called me 'my boy.' Tonight he will come again and fetch me. He promised it to me. I can bear it no longer without him."

She bent over him and her tears flowed copiously onto his bed. "My poor child!" she said and laid her hand on his forehead.

When night came she lit a lamp and watched at his bedside. He lay there quietly. He did not sleep, but stared silently before him.

He: "Mother!"

She: "What do you want, my good son?"

He: "Lay me with him in his grave! Yes? And pull the horrible stake out of his breast!"

She promised it to him with a clasp of her hand and a kiss.

He: "Oh, it must be so sweet to lie by him in the grave!"

Then midnight arrived. All at once his features were transfigured. He raised his head a bit, as if he were listening. With shining eyes he looked toward the window and the branches of the lilac bush.

"See, Mother, there he comes."

Those were his last words. Then his eyes closed. He sank back onto the pillow and died.

And she did as he had requested.

First published in Karl Heinrich Ulrichs's *Matrosengeschichten* (*Sailors' Tales*, Leipzig: F.E. Fischer, 1885); later printed separately and anthologized.
Translated from the German by Hubert Kennedy.

Moon Time
D.T. Steiner

Megan woke to the howling of wolves. Desire and revulsion tremored through her at their call. *Damn you both!* she swore. *Leave me alone!*

She remembered the beginning...

Waking to the din ... brushing shaggy brown hair away from her eyes as they flicked about the bedroom...

Milky illumination from her nightlight spilled across the floor, washed into silvery moonlight. Shadows hunched in the corners where the pale glow couldn't reach.

Megan glanced toward the window. Closed, as she'd left it. *They can't get in,* she tried to reassure herself. And thirteen was too old to be afraid of every noise in the night. Still, she trembled.

She and her mother fought an unvoiced battle over the window. Her mother usually raised it partway when she came in to tell Megan good night; Megan always shut it once her mother left.

Sometimes though, Mother would return after Megan fell asleep and reopen the window. Her mother seemed to think fresh air was as necessary as sleep.

Megan studied the room. Her large collection of dolls and stuffed animals lined the walls like faithful sentinels — from tiny Barbie to the huge panda Dad had won at the local fair after they'd moved to Forest Grove last summer.

Her eyes traveled over the group, lingering on favorites. *I'll never give you up,* she thought. *Even if I get married. You can come and be my little girl's friend.*

The wolves howled again. Megan pulled the down comforter over her head, burrowed under her pillow, and drew her knees up tight. Though the cover was almost too warm for the early fall night, she shivered.

The bedding muffled the wolves' baying and amplified her own heartbeat until it drummed over their cries. She'd yet to gather the courage to approach the window during the creatures' increasingly frequent nocturnal visits, so she hadn't actually seen them. Nor did she wish to; their calls frightened her enough.

Oddly, no one else in the family ever mentioned being awakened by the noise, though she couldn't imagine anyone sleeping through such racket.

Her father said the big old house at the edge of town had been a bargain. No wonder. Wildlife overran the place, not only wolves but raccoons, possum, rabbits, deer, and who knew what else. An old orchard, thick with blackberry brambles and tall weeds, bordered the field beyond the house. From her bedroom window, she often spotted animals there, browsing on the sweet fruits and grasses.

She'd considered asking her younger brother, Brian, if he heard the wolves, but was afraid he'd make fun of her. Brian did that too much already; no use giving him more opportunities to laugh at her.

It wasn't her fault she'd grown suddenly cranelike and ugly. Her mother's suggestion that she "start behaving like a young lady instead of a tomboy" stung more than her brother's constant teasing. Still, Megan refused to give up her t-shirts, or wear the itchy lace training bra Mom had bought her.

So what if most of the other girls in her class wore the gross thing? She preferred the freedom of cool wind through her shirt as she bicycled about after school, exploring the small town. Her skinned knees and tanned, unshaven legs were a badge of defiance against the inevitability of change.

Brushing one hand self-consciously across her chest, she felt the small bumps through her white nightgown. Her nipple hardened at the touch, and an achy twinge arced from one to the other and downward, between her legs.

Megan rubbed her thighs together to lessen the tingling, but that just intensified the sensation. She stopped, yet the insistent feeling continued to pulse through her groin. She bit her lower lip in frustration until discomfort distracted her from the throbbing.

Becoming too hot, she kicked back the covers and threw off her pillow. The howling sounded fainter, as though the wolves were moving away.

Her body twinged again. Biting her lip harder, she slipped out of bed. Her long cotton gown swished against the cool hardwood floor as she crossed the room. Pausing to scoop up a white teddy bear from his place against the wall, Megan padded to the window, halting just short of it — where she could look out but not be seen.

The orchard gleamed under the waxing moon. For a moment, Megan thought she saw a fleeting dark form at the edge of the woods beyond. Then it faded into the trees and a single howl echoed from the forest, like a feral good night from a secret admirer.

Megan dashed back across the room and jumped into bed, still clutching the bear. Jerking up the covers, she lay panting beneath them. A strange mingling of fear and excitement quivered through her, and in its wake, her body throbbed once more.

She squeezed her eyes shut, as if that would help. But she knew from experience that only one thing would quell the feeling. She kissed the teddy bear on his fuzzy lips, then held him tight while she rubbed herself until her body shuddered and finally let her sleep.

❏

"Megan!" a voice called behind her in the school hallway.

She turned and squinted through the press of students to spy her friend Gina struggling toward her. Megan smiled at her.

Gina was blonde, pretty, and what all the boys smirkingly referred to as stacked. Tall and strong, she ran on the girls' track team. Everyone seemed to like her. Though Megan had yet to figure out why someone like Gina wanted her company, their friendship made her special.

Something about Gina stirred vague, unfamiliar feelings in Megan, but she couldn't identify the emotion.

Gina reached her, giggling. "What's so funny?" Megan said.

"Jim Snyder had to go to the board in algebra with a hard-on!" Gina said, giggling again.

"Oh," Megan said, seeing no humor in the revelation.

"He was positively red!" Gina continued.

Poor Jim, Megan thought, glancing down at her chest. Even the loose sweater she wore didn't entirely hide the twin bumps that jutted forward, mocking her.

Gina greeted another friend as she and Megan walked to their mutual next class, sparing Megan the need for a reply.

As they entered the classroom, Megan found her eyes drawn as always to Mr. Lucian, the literature teacher. He stood by his desk, dressed in a black pullover and charcoal gray slacks. His thick, shining black hair reminded Megan of the ravens in the orchard at home. Obsidian eyes glittered her way, as if with some private amusement, and inky bat wing eyebrows added to his satirical expression.

Though his tall, lean-muscled frame and handsome face could have graced the cover of one of her mother's romance novels, Megan liked to imagine him as a dark knight from one of his story assignments. When he spoke, his deep, slightly accented voice seemed to vibrate with quiet power. Gina had told Megan he too was new this year.

At Megan's glance, he smiled. Feeling herself blushing under his notice, she looked away. The hotness spread downward from her face, tingling all the way to her groin. Quickly taking a seat, she opened her Lit. book and hid her face behind it.

Gina sat next to her. Poking Megan's arm, she whispered, "Isn't he gorgeous?"

Megan huddled closer to her book and didn't answer.

❏

Sighing, Megan stretched across the top of her pink down comforter. She pushed her schoolbooks over the edge of the bed, watched them fall into the circle of light from her bedside lamp. She didn't care that her homework wasn't done. Though she had always been a good student, lately she felt bored and restless.

A small, stuffed panther named Blackie lay atop her pillows. Megan picked him up and stroked his silky short fur, then reached over and turned off the lamp.

Framed by sheer pink curtains, the nearly full moon peered into her room through wispy clouds. Moonlight dappled the floor, speckling its shadow creatures, and touched Megan's body with phantom fingers.

Pulling up her nightgown, she let the moonlight silver her skin. She remembered reading an old superstition that if a girl slept naked in the moonlight she would become a witch. Giggling to herself, Megan wondered if there were any truth to the tale.

She brushed her free hand slowly over her body and then stopped, realizing what she was doing. Jerking her gown back down, she tossed the toy panther away and sat up quickly.

Blackie hit the far wall with a quiet thump and dropped to the floor. Instantly sorry, Megan hopped out of bed to retrieve him. Cradling Blackie, she caught her own reflection in the window.

Her small round face hadn't changed much, but her body appeared more gangling and grotesque with every passing day. Worst of all, her breasts were growing so fast that none of her clothing hid them any more.

As Megan stared at herself in disgust, she spotted a tall form standing in the shadows of the orchard . Though she couldn't tell which way the figure faced, she sensed eyes upon her.

She gasped and backed from the window until she bumped into the bed, then threw back the covers and jumped in, dragging the blankets to her chin. Feeling as if she were still being watched, she ducked beneath the covers with Blackie clenched in her arms.

The pleasant smells of warm cotton and down filled her nose. Soon she stopped trembling in the bed's familiar comfort. The window was shut and locked; she was safe, and maybe it had only been a trick of the shadows.

❑

She awoke to loud howling. As she scrambled from beneath the covers, her gaze froze on the gaping window. The curtains rustled in the cool breeze, and something growled, deep and low, close by.

Megan opened her mouth to scream, yet no sound escaped. She tried to move, but her body was rigid with fear. While she struggled to force herself from the bed, a black shape bounded through the window and on to the floor with a muffled thud and a skitter of claws.

Glinting eyes pierced Megan as the moon-silvered form slinked toward her. Her body remained frozen. Suddenly the wolf leaped, knocking her back against the mattress.

Giant paws held her down, crushing the breath from her. Claws raked her flesh through the thin gown. The creature's rank, warm breath mingled with her own as its eyes burned into hers.

She felt hot liquid trickle between her legs. Finally, she managed to scream. The wolf jumped from the bed, trotted to the window. It stopped, looked toward her, and whined like a dog. All Megan could do was stare at it in terror.

The wolf whined once more, its gaze seeming somehow pleading, then sprang out the window.

The door flew open. Her mother hurried in, flipping on the table lamp as she neared the bed. Megan drew a ragged breath and began to sob.

"What's wrong, honey?" her mother asked.

Megan just gaped at her, still sobbing and unable to speak.

Her mother sat to brush a hand through Megan's tangled hair. "You screamed, baby. Did you have a nightmare?"

Megan glanced fearfully toward the window, back at her mother. "There was a wolf. He wanted to hurt me."

"Honey, you were dreaming." Her mother stroked her hair again.

Noticing a damp, uncomfortable feeling, Megan realized she'd wet her bed. Her cheeks flushed with embarrassment. "I ... I'm all right now."

"Sure?"

"Yes." Megan tried to smile. "But would you close the window? I'm cold."

Her mother did it without argument, then crossed to the door. Turning back to Megan, she said, "If you need me, just call."

"I will."

Once her mother shut the door, Megan jumped up and ran to lock the window. She nervously scanned the grounds, but the area seemed deserted. The moon silvered the landscape like one of those metallic pictures she'd seen at the mall.

Megan still felt as if something were watching her from the shadowy woods. Jerking the curtains free of their tiebacks, she pulled them over the window before going to clean up.

As she lifted the soiled gown over her head, she saw short claw marks on her chest. She thought of showing them to her mother, but imagined Mom claiming she'd only scratched herself in her sleep.

Megan felt a surge of unfamiliar resentment; if her mother hadn't opened the window, nothing would've happened. She decided to have a talk with Mom and insist on control over her own room.

But would that keep the wolf out? Megan eyed the window uncertainly. Even locking it was no guarantee of safety. The old single-paned glass rattled in every wind; if the wolf wanted in badly enough, that thin barrier was no protection.

She considered nailing some boards over the window, but discarded the idea. How could she explain that to her parents?

Megan glanced about the room. Her dresser was tall enough to block the bottom half of the window. That might help. After slipping on a clean nightgown, she began dragging the heavy oak chest across the floor.

The dresser legs squeaked against the hardwood, leaving skid marks in their wake, and Megan feared the noise would bring her mother back. Then again, if everyone else slept through wolf howls, a little midnight furniture moving shouldn't disturb them.

Megan shoved the dresser in front of the window. The bottom sill kept the chest inches from the glass, but she hoped the barricade would at least allow her to escape before the wolf could reach her.

She stripped the bed, placing a towel over the wet spot, put on clean sheets, and hid the soiled laundry deep in the hall hamper. Then she filled the gap where the dresser had stood with her dolls and stuffed animals before climbing back into bed with her white teddy bear.

Leaving on the light, she tried to sleep, but kept opening her eyes to check the window every few moments. Nothing further happened, yet dawn broke before she felt safe enough to close her eyes.

The day was sunny, with just a hint of fall crispness. Megan and Gina walked toward Main Street, leaves crackling beneath their sneakers. The air smelled of burning leaves and wood smoke, and the trees bordering the way were brilliant with yellows, rust, and scarlets.

They were headed for Forest Grove's yearly Harvest Fair celebration. Booths of goods, foods, and craft exhibits lined Main Street from the town square to the edge of the commercial district. As they neared the site, Megan's mouth watered at the mingled odors drifting from the food vendors' booths.

The area was crowded with locals and a small number of tourists. Laughter and delighted screams rose from the small carnival that filled the far section of the street.

Megan absently twirled a strand of hair round one finger as she and Gina browsed through the festival site.

"Are you going to the street dance tonight?" Gina asked.

"I don't think so," Megan said.

"Oh, come on," Gina said. "It'll be fun. You can go with me."

"Don't you have a date?" Megan asked in surprise.

Gina laughed. "Why should I limit myself to one partner? There'll be plenty of guys to dance with."

Noticing how Gina's hair shone like pale silk in the sunlight, Megan wished she could touch it. The thought embarrassed her, and she turned her attention to a booth of jewelry.

Drawing beside her, Gina picked up a silver necklace of a crescent moon within a circle. Placing the necklace over Megan's head, she said, "It's like you. Swelling, but not complete yet."

Uncertain of Gina's meaning, Megan looked away.

"Will you come to the dance with me?" Gina said.

Megan felt herself blushing. "I ... I guess so," she stammered.

Fingers brushed Megan's throat as Gina removed the necklace, the contact sending a ticklish feeling shivering through Megan. She started toward the next booth to take her mind from the sensation.

Gina followed, and their talk turned to other subjects. As they strolled among the booths, Megan felt as if she were being watched. She kept glancing about, but could never catch anyone studying her.

While Gina went for a Coke, Megan stopped at a table of handmade stuffed animals. A few moments later she sensed someone stepping up behind her. Thinking Gina was sneaking up on her, she pivoted with a giggle, the laugh ending in a gasp as she realized her mistake.

Mr. Lucian smiled down at her. His eyes glittered with their usual amusement, and something else that Megan couldn't identify. His gaze made her uncomfortable and fidgety. Confused, Megan lowered her eyes and played with her hands.

"You look lovely today," Mr. Lucian said.

Megan glanced up at him, then about the crowded street for any sign of Gina. Her friend had disappeared from sight, and Megan could feel Mr. Lucian's eyes still upon her.

"Thank you," she managed, looking back at him. His intense gaze burned into her. The sounds of the festival faded around her — until she was aware only of his stare and the thud of her own heartbeat.

Feeling like a rabbit captured in the grip of some wild animal, she had a fleeting mental image of being held between massive jaws.

Just then Gina returned. She giggled when she saw who was with Megan. "Hi, Mr. Lucian," she said. "Are you enjoying the fair?"

"Very much so, Gina," he said, fixing her with the same look and smile he had given Megan. "And yourself?"

She laughed. "I always have fun, Mr. Lucian."

"Good. That's what youth and vitality are for." He eyed Megan once more. "Don't you agree, Megan?"

Avoiding his scrutiny, she murmured, "I guess so."

"I'll see you girls later then," he said, starting away.

"Megan's got a boyfriend!" Gina teased with a laugh.

Megan stuck out her tongue at Gina, then marched away. Catching up, Gina slipped an arm through hers, and the two giggled together.

"Have you ever had a special boyfriend?" Megan asked seriously.

Gina smiled like a fox. "Maybe."

"Did you go steady and all?"

"All what?"

"You know," Megan whispered.

Gina smiled slyly again. "Maybe I'll tell you about it someday." She leaned closer as if to whisper something, her warm breath tickling Megan's ear, and added, "When you're blooded."

"What do you mean?" Megan said. "I'm already having periods."

"Later," Gina said. Waving to a boy from school, she hurried toward him, dragging Megan along.

❑

Megan walked along the park footpath next to Gina, the full moon illuminating their way through the trees. Though she tried not to, Megan kept thinking about wolves, and imagining she saw movement in every shadow.

Gina didn't seem nervous, but one of the beasts hadn't leapt on *her* the other night. Megan wanted to tell her about it, but figured Gina would echo her mother by saying she'd only been dreaming.

The two talked quietly about the dance. Despite a few awkward moments, Megan had enjoyed herself. Mr. Lucian even showed up for a while. Megan was surprised when he'd asked Gina and several other girls to dance during the slow numbers.

While he held each partner at a proper distance as he twirled her about the street, Megan got an eerie impression of some dark force pursuing them all in a spiral game of hunter and hunted.

Then he'd asked Megan to dance. Though his grip was strong, his hands tremored as if he were holding some emotion in check. His body felt hot, and his black eyes appeared almost feverish. His gaze locked on hers as though no one else existed.

Embarrassed, Megan tried to look away, found she couldn't. The music and people around them faded, as if she and Mr. Lucian danced in a private place.

A flush of excitement warmed her face, stole through her body, intensified into a familiar throbbing between her legs. Megan attempted to ignore it, but by the time the song ended, wished she were home in bed — where she could satisfy her body's demands.

Mr. Lucian thanked her and then disappeared among the other couples. Megan didn't see him again.

Later, Gina danced a few fast numbers with her. While sexual tension kept Megan too distracted to really focus on her friend, she had been pleased by Gina's attention.

As if reading her thoughts, Gina smiled at Megan as they neared the edge of the park. "Would you like to see something special?" Gina asked.

"What?" Megan said.

Drawing her off the path, Gina paused in the shadow of a tall fir. Megan's gaze darted about. "I don't think we should stop here," she said.

Gina's white teeth shone in the moonlight. "What are you afraid of? Me?"

"Don't be silly!" Megan said.

"Maybe you should be," Gina said softly.

Megan stared at her, ready to tell Gina to quit teasing. But something in the other's eyes froze her reply, an alien look Megan had never seen there before.

Then Gina laughed and the look vanished. She leaned closer, brushing her lips against Megan's. A shock went through Megan, and with it, sharp pleasure. Megan closed her eyes as the feeling spasmed through her.

"Maybe I'm gonna eat you all up," Gina whispered.

Megan shivered. She didn't know what to think. Was Gina playing a cruel joke on her? She felt fascinated, repelled, and afraid all at once.

As Gina nuzzled her neck, Megan opened her eyes again. She was about to draw away when she spotted a dark shape bounding toward them through the trees.

Megan pushed Gina away so hard she knocked her to the ground. "Gina, run!" Megan cried.

She pulled Gina to her feet before bolting away in blind panic. Somehow she knew the creature wanted her alone.

Racing headlong through the trees, Megan glanced behind her, screamed when she discovered two wolves chasing her. Moonlight dappled their coats, one black, like her attacker from the other night, the second a tawny color.

The wolves were gaining. Megan veered back toward open ground but the beasts angled to cut her off, steering her deeper into the woods. Her heart pounded painfully as she strained for air, and tears stung her eyes.

The wolves herded her in ever-shrinking spirals until she dropped from exhaustion. Cringing into a ball, she lay sobbing and gasping for air, eyes squeezed tight against the horror, waiting for the wolves to attack.

She heard their panting breaths, even above her own, sensed their hungry stares, imagined their long fangs piercing her flesh. Nothing happened for what seemed like minutes, then Megan felt not claws or teeth but hands trying to roll her over. She resisted.

"It's all right, Megan," Gina said. "No one's going to hurt you. Trust me."

Daring a glance, Megan saw Gina kneeling beside her, naked, long blonde hair brushing the full breasts. Despite her fear, Megan noticed how pink and erect her friend's nipples were in the moonlight.

Gina smiled and stroked Megan's hair. Seeing a movement behind Gina, Megan froze. The black wolf stood nearby, tongue lolling, its glittering eyes fixed on Megan.

"He won't harm you," Gina said. "I promise. Look."

She stretched one hand back to the wolf and it padded forward to let her pet it. "Now you touch him," she said.

Megan shook her head, but the wolf approached slowly, then halted beside Gina. Meeting the creature's gaze, Megan thought she recognized something familiar in the wolf's eyes.

Fear warred with curiosity inside her. Before she realized it, she reached out to pat the wolf, found its fur surprisingly soft.

The wolf's velvety tongue flicked across Megan's hand. She gasped and recoiled at the unexpected action.

"I told you he wouldn't hurt you," Gina said.

Leaning down, she kissed Megan tenderly on the lips. At the same time, Megan felt the wolf lick her cheek.

Repulsion and excitement quivered through her at their alien touches.

Gina kissed her again and began to caress her. Megan closed her eyes wondering whether it would do any good if she begged Gina to quit — or even if she wanted her friend to stop.

Hands started undoing her blouse. Megan's eyes and mouth flew open in protest. But her words died as she found herself staring up into Mr. Lucian's riveting black gaze.

Smiling at her, he cupped her face in one hand, then caressed her cheek. A shiver coursed down her spine, mingled fright and pleasure, and her cheeks burned with shame at what he must have seen.

Finally, she managed to gasp, "Mr. Lucian, what are you doing here?"

He continued smiling while he finished unbuttoning her shirt. Terror unfroze her body. Rolling away, she scrambled to her feet and stumbled off. An unearthly howl echoed behind her.

Sobbing, she ran blindly through the trees. Soon she heard snarls, and dry leaves crackling under loping paws. The sounds of pursuit grew louder.

Suddenly, something struck her from behind, sent her sprawling. Before Megan could stagger up, the black wolf leapt on her. She screamed as its teeth sank into one arm.

Pain seared her flesh. The wolf released her, but the pain spread through her like wildfire. Waves of dizziness and nausea swept over her. Helpless to escape, she curled into a ball once more.

Her body glistened with clammy sweat, began to shake violently. She cried out, was answered by wolf howls from the two circling beasts. She felt her bones shifting and pulling, as if to break her skin.

A final scream, then conscious thought was ripped from her in a thrashing frenzy of agony and change.

Gradually, the pain lessened. Megan lay on her side, exhausted. She opened her eyes, but her vision was oddly different.

The night looked brighter than it had, yet the world was cast in shades of gray. Every sound seemed amplified many times, and a hundred smells overwhelmed her nose.

Nearby, the two wolves watched her. A strange whine came from her throat. She struggled up, stood swaying and disoriented. Something was horribly wrong.

She glanced at the ground, saw her two feet — misshapen and covered with brown fur. Her scream erupted from her throat as a yelp of fear.

Part of her shrank away, to a safe, dark place deep in her mind.

The black wolf trotted forward to lick her face. Another part of her licked back. He jumped up, pawing her, playing.

The tawny wolf joined in. The three played together for a few moments, then the black wolf led them off through the woods at a lope.

❏

Megan awoke slowly. Morning sunlight streamed in through her pink curtains. Squinting against the brightness, she discovered that she lay naked across her made bed.

She yawned and stretched, but stopped as sore muscles twitched and jerked. Her small breasts ached, and she felt as if her period were about to start, though it wasn't due yet.

She sensed a wrongness about her body. Somehow she didn't feel right; when she examined herself, she found long red scratches everywhere and bruises purple with the imprint of bite marks.

Fear shot through her. What had happened? She didn't remember coming home last night — in fact, didn't recall anything after leaving the dance. Her gaze flicked to the window. Shut and locked, the dresser still guarding it.

Despite that reassurance, she felt suddenly sick to her stomach. As she scrambled from the bed, one foot slipped on something soft and furry. She glanced down, gasped at what she saw. Her favorite white teddy bear had been torn limb from limb, his stuffing scattered across the floor.

Megan sobbed. Kneeling, she gathered up the pieces, clutching them to her. Just then her stomach heaved, and she vomited on the bear's strewn cotton insides.

When the sickness passed, she collapsed back on the bed and drew up her knees, still holding the bear's pieces, too weak to clean up the mess.

A dark wetness stained the bed where she had first lain. At that instant, an image flashed through her brain. One hand flew to her mouth to smother the scream.

In her mind's eye, two wolves loped through the forest, one black, one tawny. Her view of the scene seemed distorted, until she perceived *she* was running at the same speed and low angle — realized with horror that she had to be with them.

She strained to retrace events after the dance. She and Gina were walking through the park when...

Her mind shrank from the memory. She forced it back. She had to know.

As she kept returning to the moments she last remembered, other snatches of imagery appeared. Gina kissing her ... kneeling over her, naked ... Mr. Lucian touching her. A black wolf chasing her ... biting her! Pain ... change. Change to *what?*

Megan shuddered, recoiled from the vague dark shape forming in her thoughts. Whatever occurred had involved Gina and Mr. Lucian.

Talking to the teacher would be too embarrassing, but Megan was surprised Gina hadn't already called *her*. She wondered if her friend's recollections were as shadowy as her own, or if Gina might wish to avoid her now out of embarrassment.

Or maybe Gina hadn't called for a more gruesome reason. What if the wolves had killed her?

Stumbling up, Megan rushed to her phone and pushed Gina's number. After several rings, her friend answered.

"Gina, this is Megan! Are you all right?"

The other laughed. "Of course. Why wouldn't I be?"

Megan debated how to answer. Finally, she stammered, "Don't you remember ... what happened last night?"

Gina replied with a question of her own. "What do you remember?"

"I ... Gina, please. Tell me."

"I remember how good you smelled ... and tasted."

Megan gasped, then clamped her hand over the receiver to hide a sob.

"Are you there, Megan?" Gina asked.

She uncovered the receiver, but couldn't speak.

"Let me come over and talk to you," Gina said. "I can't explain things on the phone."

"All right," Megan whispered and quickly hung up.

❑

"Gina, what *happened* last night?" Megan said as her bedroom door closed behind them.

"You're one of us now," Gina said. "Don't you feel it?"

She touched Megan's shoulder, but Megan flinched from the contact. Her voice shook when she spoke. "I don't feel anything! What do you mean, one of us? Who?"

"Lucian and I."

Megan looked away in shame. "Mr. Lucian?" So it hadn't been some horrible nightmare; he'd seen everything, had...

Repelled, she pushed the memory away. All she could manage was a weak "Why?"

"Lucian desired you. And so did I."

Confused, and still unable to meet Gina's steady gaze, Megan said, "I don't understand."

"Lucian is different. He can change into other forms. And he's shared that power with you and me."

Dark scenes of running wolves tormented Megan. Whirling on Gina, she cried, "I don't want it!"

"I felt that way too, at first. But you'll like being able to change once you get used to it. Trust me, Megan. I wouldn't hurt you."

"Get out!" Megan shouted. "I hate you!"

"No, you don't," Gina said softly. "And you can't. We're sisters of the same blood now."

Megan flung herself onto the bed sobbing. "Just go."

"Come to me when you're ready," Gina said. "I can help you."

Megan cried harder as the door shut behind Gina. She knew Gina was at least half right. Part of her did hate her friend for what she had done, but another part couldn't. She sensed an alteration, a bond other than friendship linking them, something almost instinctive. But worst of all, she felt the change in herself as well, an alienness deep within.

❏

The wolves howled again. Megan got out of bed, restless as their cries stirred her. She felt the internal shifting begin, as if some black beast were uncoiling itself from her center. Waking ... eager to live anew.

Her gaze fixed automatically on the window. She'd dragged the dresser away from it months ago. Sighing, she padded over and looked out. Even through the glass, she could smell the night.

Moonlight glittered on the deep whiteness blanketing the ground below. The winter evening was hushed, wrapped in the snow's cold embrace. Soft, powder snow — easy to run on — that crunched beneath brown paws like small bones breaking.

She closed her eyes as dark images flickered through her mind like a faintly remembered dream. She'd wanted to tell her family what had happened to her, but shame, and a stronger instinct, for survival, kept her silent.

And other emotions were involved. Gina roused feelings in her she didn't understand. But apart from her confusing inner turmoil, she could never betray Gina. They were sisters of the night, sharing blood and bodies.

Her feelings toward Lucian were mixed. He was pack leader, and her mentor. Her dark twin would have given its life for him; her rational mind hated him for altering her forever.

She pressed her cheek against the chill windowpane. Her body shook as the wildness within tore at her control. Even if she didn't want the change, it was happening, as inevitable as the full moon. As inescapable as growing up.

She heard a yap and a whine, opened her eyes. Across the ice-sparkled field, two forms raced toward her. Gina and Lucian were coming. And then moon time would begin its cycle once more.

Imagined
Jay B. Laws

1

He was everything I'd imagined. He was everything I was not.

"How'd you get here?" I kept asking him.

"Does it really matter?" He grinned at me in the dark. Rubbed his chest with his hands. His fingers brushed against the sweep of dark curly hair crowning each pink nipple, toying with himself.

That first night he slid his hands under my ass, a hand for each cheek, and took me. His broad shoulders showcased his upper half into a perfect V-shape, while his middle torso was hard and satin smooth. A thick mat of black hair, ridiculously rectangular, urged my downcast eyes to stare at what hung like an indolent knight asleep before battle. He traced maps of where he'd been along my spine, each whispery contact of his coarse fingers spreading delicious shivers through me. Later, when he dozed — his body was short, compact, evenly matched with mine, down to the toes wrapped between my own — I thought that it *did* matter, his presence here with me. Our lovemaking had left us exhausted, salty, and content. But an odor hung in the dark air like an afterthought, the smell of sulfur and fire and of worlds colliding. I pulled him closer.

2

I first noticed his cigarettes. A sure giveaway. I think he wanted to tease me. I'd come home from my days at the temp agencies and find cigarette butts in the ashtray.

My roommate George: "Don't look at *me*. I don't smoke Camels."

I knew who did. But I didn't say anything.

Late at night, after dinner, T.V., I'd pull up the typewriter. This is where I'd first made Rob's acquaintance a few weeks earlier. He was a master of sexual technique, charming and gracious, with a generous ten-inch package. A swarthy Italian, great furry thighs, enormous hands. The kind of piercing green eyes that pin you to the truth. All right, I'll admit it: I wasn't too original, conjuring up this man of my dreams. "Swarthy" Italian. "Ten-inch" package. I was trying to earn extra money writing porno stories. I wanted to push all the right buttons for *me*. So at night when I lay in bed and grasped myself with both hands, it was *his* image that floated before my feverish eyes. We were in the shower together at a gym, he coach and me student with a calf needing a massage. He was the hitchhiker stranded on a northern California road. The army private. The burglar. The fireman. The man in the window across the street as he slipped out of his jock strap.

And in the morning, or late at night before bed, I'd pound out our story on the typewriter, hoping that eventually I'd write something good enough to sell. But alone in the darkness of my bedroom I used to think, If ever a man could satisfy me, it'd be Rob. If only he'd come see me. He was the perfect playmate. Real men couldn't compare. Real men weren't even competition.

Rob must have noticed. He must have known how I felt.

One evening I went to the typewriter and saw the message he'd left for me.

I want to come see you.

The next day when George found the cigarette butts, I knew it was only a matter of time before Rob showed himself.

I'd take a shower and catch a swift movement out of the corner of my eye.

I'd walk into the apartment at night and hear the rocking chair squeak to a sudden halt.

The notes became insistent.

Let me come see you.

I thought you wanted me.

And then, the final capper:

I'll teach you how to get fucked.

I looked at what Rob had written and felt a trembling warmth flood through me. My breath grew shallow. He had culled my deepest, darkest secret from a place in my mind even I had kept hidden, even to myself. He knew how complicated it had become in the real world. Surely, Rob would be different. He *had* to be different. Feeling an unprecedented excitement, I sat at the typewriter, hit the return, and typed:

Okay, Rob. You win. I'll give it a try.

Underneath my fingers the typewriter whirled into life. I say underneath; my fingers touched not one key. Yet I wasn't surprised when the words stacked one upon the other in rapid succession.

Good. How about tonight?

I panicked. *No, Rob.*

Why not? I know you want me.

I don't know if I want dreams come true.

That shut him up. The typewriter purred with electricity but held back its secrets.

I tried to finish "Daddy's Revenge" but Rob wouldn't cooperate. He couldn't keep his hard-on — he *wouldn't* keep his hard-on — and he sulked. Dwight, the Omaha runaway who shared the barn with Rob, stroked the ten inches with his lips, pulled on his balls, pinched his nipples — but Rob ignored him. Finally I couldn't take his insolence.

Listen here, I typed, *if you're going to be so goddamned stubborn then get the hell out of my story.*

Rob looked away from Dwight and smiled up from the twenty-pound bond paper.

With pleasure.

3

That night he came to my bed. I reached for the lamp but he stopped me.

"I like it better in the dark," Rob said. His voice was husky and rough, like warm flannel. I sighed with anticipation.

"I want to look at you," I said. "Really look at you, in the light."

"You can't. I'm sorry."

I was about to protest when his hands reached expertly for my briefs and slid them down past my ankles and off with one luxurious motion. His lips found my right nipple. His tongue darted and whipped. His tickling moustache rocketed me to heaven when he flipped me over and licked between my cheeks with his tongue. I wanted to tell him to stop, that we weren't supposed to do that anymore because it wasn't safe, but since he was of my imagination, I figured he'd be all right.

Rob leaned back against the headboard and spread his furry legs across the sheets. His left hand grasped his gigantic manhood while his right hand massaged his pecs and tweaked a plum-colored nipple. "I think it's time we got down to business. You'll enjoy yourself."

"Promise?"

"If you don't," he whispered, "I'll *make* you like it."

I looked at Rob's shadowy outline in my bedroom darkness and let a hand fall to my hard-on. It was so swollen it bobbed up and down by itself.

Rob jerked himself madly with both hands. Two hands, and still he extended up and over those fingers. His hands were a blur.

"Don't," I rasped. "Save it for me."

Abruptly Rob stopped. "There's plenty more where this comes from," he bragged, smiling. He scooped me against him. "And you've waited long enough." He found the lube on the nightstand and massaged my ass with his hand. I let myself breathe deeper, deeper. "I know you have trouble with real people, but I'm different. We can do anything we want. See?" As if to prove his point, he pushed the tip of his erection into me. "Relax. That's it." He began to jerk me off as he probed deeper. A cool sweat oiled our skin. It still hurt.

"Wait—"

"No can do, buddy. Sink or swim."

He slapped against me, his hands pulling me against him with each thrust. Something began to thaw, then melt. It began at my groin and spiraled deliciously throughout my body. By the time it had traveled to my tongue, it spilled out as one continuous moan after another. I was sinking *and* swimming.

"Will you go away in the morning?" I gasped.

"Yes. But I'll come back each night." And with that, he dug his long moist tongue into my ear.

"Oh god! Oh god — I think I'm—"

I came in a great gush, shooting all over the sheets. With a grunt Rob pulled out and streaked my stomach and chest in hot white ribbons. He collapsed against me, both of us laughing at the spasms that still choked us.

When I awoke in the morning to full sunlight, only his scent remained, and a few curly hairs against the sheets.

4

I stopped my work with the temporary agencies downtown and spent my days in front of the typewriter. At night, in darkness, we shaped the plots of Rob's stories.

"No, I wouldn't go after Larry, the water boy," he'd growl. "Give me the coach." And so the next day, sitting at the typewriter in my gym shorts, last night's fantasy became tomorrow's hopeful paycheck. I had Rob fearlessly plunder the willing football coach as eight players stood round and cheered him on.

The stories piled up: "Uncle's Well-Kept Secret," "A Night in Blue Heaven," and my personal favorite, "Under the Windowsill." On impulse I sent the first one to one of those glossy magazines with pictures of California blonds, and when they bought it asking for more, Rob and I shared a bottle of French champagne and licked ripe red grapes out of each other's belly buttons.

5

George got worried.

"You're not working," he said. "You're not socializing. Why are you staying up so late?"

"I'm writing."

"I don't hear the typewriter."

"I'm writing the first draft in long hand."

George frowned. "Who's your friend?"

"What are you talking about?" I knew how to play coy when I had to.

"Look: I know someone comes in here. You should tell your buddy not to leave cigarette butts all over the house. Are you ashamed of him? Is that it? Or does he visit you when he's supposed to be somewhere else?"

I smiled. "Something like that."

Another frown. George was always big on frowns. "You know he'll eventually dump you, if he's seeing you on the side. They always do."

"Not Rob."

Damn. That slipped out. One of George's eyebrows did a funny dance. I watched him grope for the next words.

"You mean — Rob, like the guy in your dirty stories?"

I stared at George, my shoulders squared.

"Sure."

His expression was priceless.

6

Rob wasn't so amused.

"You shouldn't have told!" he whined. "It's against all the rules."

"Don't worry. He won't believe me. Shoot — I still don't believe it all myself. And against *what* rules?"

Rob stormed around the bedroom. I'd never seen him so agitated. "You think it's easy for me to come here every night? It breaks the rules."

"What rules?"

Rob folded his big arms across his naked chest. He stared at me like I was an idiot. "The rules that govern *everything!*"

That shut me up. I guess I'd known deep down that Rob's presence here bent somebody's rules, but I hadn't wanted to dwell upon it.

Rob's anger abruptly yielded to a more urgent need; he was unpredictable that way. He flipped me onto my stomach and slapped at the round bubble of my ass. "But enough talking." His fingers began to massage and probe. He pushed my legs apart and grabbed at the tufts of hair directly under my balls.

"Wait a minute. Slow down," I commanded. His getting mad at me had made me defiant. "Let me turn on a light this time."

"What for?" Now a rough hand cupped my balls, tugging and squeezing with one perfect motion. Despite myself, a low moan escaped my clenched lips.

"Rob, wait. I want to see you — *really* see you." For the truth was, even with all our bedroom gymnastics, not once had a bedside lamp or morning sun or even light spilled from a doorway's crack spoiled the complete darkness that swallowed our midnight lovemaking. Only my mind's eye added dimension and detail to what was in reality a darker shadow carved from a room in shadow.

"No."

"Then let me up. I don't want to do this."

At that moment he slid two greased fingers into me. "Oh yes you do," he said, pumping his hand callously. "You brought me here but now you'll do as I say." He pinned my arms straight out in front of my head and leaned his full weight against me. His stiff weapon banged against the crack of my ass. He oiled himself with spit. "It's okay," he purred, trying to soften his tune. "You'll like this." He entered me, painfully, withdrew once, and entered again. "Look," he whispered, finding his rhythm, "this isn't so bad. We can do anything we want. All that's asked in return is that you not see me. So don't spoil it."

I closed my eyes, enduring.

"Of course, you know," he added casually, "if you try to break the rules, I'll have to bring you back with me."

A chill, like leaves scattered by an October wind, shivered through me.

"You'd enjoy it there. No roommates sticking their nose where it doesn't belong. The best sex you could ever hope for, night and day. Of course, it *is* a little flat there."

"Rob: what would happen If I *did* see you?"

Rob stopped his thrusting.

"Well?"

"Shut up. Just shut up — okay?" He pumped me with renewed gusto. I squeezed my eyes shut and looked into the darkness behind my eyelids. This darkness had a shape, riding me with hands and tongue and cock, riding me, I didn't know where, this darkness that I had created and could no longer control.

7

From that moment I became clearheaded with purpose.

I cornered George in the kitchen and gave it to him straight. His face remained motionless, but every once in a while he scratched his chin thoughtfully or stared off into space.

"Listen," I growled impatiently. "I don't care if you believe me or not. All I want you to do is turn on the light tonight while he and I are in bed. Deal?"

George shook his head.

"Sorry. I've got a date tonight. You're on your own."

8

And so I waited for nightfall. Rob's words echoed in my mind.

If you try to break the rules, I'll have to bring you back with me.

He arrived promptly at eight. I had walked into the bedroom one last time to double-check my plan when I felt hands grab me from behind.

"You're early," I said, trying not to reveal the fears crowding my mind.

"Why wait for bedtime?" Rob chuckled. His hands roamed my muscular build in sweeping circles. "See? Why would you want to give this up for real life? It's better this way, just the two of us, in the dark. Now take off your clothes."

I stepped away from him and unbuttoned my flannel shirt. I kicked sneakers into the corner and pulled off my

501s with an awkward dance that made him grin. My shirt joined the pile of clothes tossed into the corner. Naked, I knelt before him. I knew what I had to do, one last time. I reached for his belt buckle.

"That's right. Pull it out of those jeans. Who cares if you can't see it? Now go for it."

Rob cupped my head in his big hands and pushed me against him. For a moment I thought, This is good, this is like before, this is how it should have stayed — but then those thoughts were pounded away by the gyrating motion of Rob slapping himself against my stretched lips. He gurgled and cooed like a satisfied baby. I worked him over until his groans were steady.

"Okay," I whispered, taking him out of my mouth and into my hands, "come to bed." I led him over to my bed, where he slipped out of his clothes. As soon as he was naked he pushed me onto the mattress. He kissed me with a surprising hunger that stirred my own passion, even as I knew what had to be done. His tongue slid across my hairy chest and worked down the soft line of fur to my crotch. He brushed my erection with his lips, sinking lower to take not one but both of my balls into his warm mouth.

"Uh-huh. Uh-huhhh," I gushed with genuine gusto. Anything to hide what I was about to do.

I reached above my head, sliding my hands up the mattress, toward the pillows. I checked under the first one. Nothing. Stretching further, I found the other pillow and swept my hand underneath with one clean motion. Nothing. Suddenly I felt very cold.

Rob let my balls plop out of his mouth.

"Something wrong?" he sneered.

"Uh — no. Nothing. Don't stop."

"No, I don't suppose you want me to stop. Not until you've found your little surprise. But that's okay," he said, shaking something that rattled like metal against metal, "I took the liberty of finding it for you."

My heart sank.

"We've no secrets, you and I," he said, unscrewing the cap from the flashlight. Two cold batteries fell against my stomach and rolled onto the bed. He screwed the cap back on. "Maybe I should fuck you with this. Would you like that? Teach you a lesson."

Abruptly he grabbed a leg with each of his powerful arms and scooted me against him. He reached for the lubricant on the end table and greased himself up. "I think I'll take you back with me tonight," he said, entering me. I gasped as I felt him push me apart. "Better yet, why don't we trade places for a while. I'm beginning to like this real world." He leaned against me cruelly, crushing me into the soft mattress.

A dull excitement began to take hold of me. Stars exploded somewhere in my head as he worked in and out, pumping me with his selfish rhythm. Over. It was all over, my plan, my life. I was going to go with him.

And I thought, When he comes, I'll probably just be swallowed up and disappear. He'll take me with him, and I won't have the strength to fight.

That weird excitement ran through me again.

Rob's pounding increased. "This is for trying to pull a fast one, you little creep! Uh-huh! Uh-huh! I'm—"

The room exploded with white light. Instantly the smell of sulfur and smoke stung the air. My head was turned at an angle toward the bedroom door. I had just enough time to glimpse a startled George blinking against the smoke before I looked away and focused deliberately on Rob.

Or on what was left of him.

He had frozen into a sort of instant Polaroid, muscles clenched in the throes of orgasm as he emptied his load deep inside me. In the white light of the overhead lamp his face registered total surprise: jaw slack and loose, eyes big as an owl's, a stunned circle for a mouth. I was prepared for that.

I wasn't prepared for what Rob looked like.

He was a cartoon. Or, more exactly, a thing of ink, a hollow outline, an artist's sketch. In the dark, Rob was heavy and muscular and hairy. In the light he transformed into what he had been all along: lines and angles and air.

We stared at each other. We had just enough time for that. And then, starting at the top of his body with his face, he began to crumble, his charcoalish outline snapping like dry twigs in a fire, crumbling, so that by the time he would have normally fallen against me, he floated as black snowflakes onto my skin. Ash rained down in a tiny storm over my thighs, stomach, and crotch.

George fainted dead away.

Ferata

Kij Johnson

I dream about Mike every day, as I sleep in my hot, airless bedroom. Sometimes we fight, and still shouting he rapes me, and I feel the stove coil burning into my back and the pain of his thrusting, just the way it was. Sometimes it's different: Mike's out on the asphalt apron outside, and he tears through the flimsy lock and into my room, his anger an iron to brand me.

This time he's in the bathroom. He's managed to get through the little frosted window in the corner shower stall — I know this is crazy, but I believe it implicitly — and now he's standing naked in the cubicle, surrounded by wet towels. I can see how his broad foot splays against the cracked concrete, one muscled buttock propping him up on the sink.

I jerk awake, my eyes staring up through the shadows to the cheap plaster ceiling. It's dark already. The clock glows aqua: 1:38. The alarm didn't go off at eight, and I've slept into the night. Now I am alone in the dark, and Mike's in the bathroom, waiting. I listen for the silence that will prove this was just another dream, but my heart beats too hard to hear above its crashing. Groping for the sewing scissors under my pillow, I sob, "Goddammit, get it over with," and lunge out of bed toward the bathroom, the shears held like a knife in my hand.

There is no one there. The bathroom is dark, the old white porcelain of the sink and toilet glowing softly in the dim light from the tiny window. My stomach wrenches with unused adrenaline; dropping the scissors into the sink, I drop to the floor, throwing up again and again until the muscles are exhausted. After a while I am done, and I rest my face against the damp, sweating box of the toilet.

Outside, a car door opens and feet crunch on gravel. In a fresh panic, I snatch on the dirty sundress that lies by my bed, and then, remembering my scars, pull a long-sleeved blouse over that. The fabric grabs at my sweaty skin. I want to throw up again, but there's no time, he might be at the door already. I run out into the little yard in front of my place, the scissors in my hand.

My home is so small in the pink-edged light of the streetlamp out in the alley. It used to be a gas station, and it hunches, a sullen heap of concrete blocks, in front of a cracked asphalt apron. When Mike and I moved in, it seemed very amusing.

The car did not come here. My yard is filled only with shadows and the dark hulk of my Buick. There are more footsteps on gravel, but they are next door, and I hear young Hispanic voices over the tall wall and the hiss of a beer can opening. Dust grinds under my fingers when I open the car door, sticks to my legs when I sit on the dirty vinyl seat. The car starts reluctantly.

It is quiet at Vic's, right between the last drunks going home and the first junkies coming down from their evening fix.

"Hey, Ell." Tony dives into the kitchen with an arm of plates. "With you in a minute." The steel-plated door swings open behind him, and for a moment I catch the sizzle and the smoky smell of the grill. I flinch and sit down at the linoleum counter, away from the swinging door. When Tony swings back out again, he grabs a cup and a coppery plastic pot and slams them down beside me.

It's the usual crowd, a few men in dirty shirts and stained boots off a late shift somewhere, three teenage boys in painted street leathers, a table of women in parrot-colored dresses and men in dinner jackets smoking imported cigarettes. I take the last for slumming royalty.

The coffee is terrible and bites into my stomach with sour teeth. My hands shake when I pour, but I drink the stuff anyway, fighting my exhaustion. My back aches, and my mouth tastes bitter. The coffee pot is empty.

"Tony?" He is behind the counter a few feet away from me, leaning against the Coke dispenser, but he doesn't move. His eyes are glazed, staring at the diner's door behind me. I swivel on my stool.

She sways in the open door, a white woman in a red dress. The pavement releases the day's heat in waves that make the car behind her weave in the blue streetlight. It is a red Corvette with tinted black windows and California license plates that say FERATA.

She is well over six feet tall. Her lush figure is wrapped in a red leather sheath, high-necked and sleeveless, with an oversize black belt around her waist. Apart from that, she is dead white, with platinum hair and icy skin. I can see the blue of veins in her temples. Her lips and fingernails show crimson, but I guess that underneath the makeup they are as white as the rest of her, maybe even pale blue. Her eyes will be pink, but they hide behind black wraparound sunglasses that give an illusion of depth, like a gash of dead water between ice floes.

She walks slowly to the counter a few stools from me and orders a coffee. Tony jerks upright from his slouch and rings her a cup without appearing to see her, then returns to his position against the machine, the same lost look on his face.

I look around. The street kids hunch around the table, their voices torrents of low, fierce Spanish. Several men sit alone at the counter with coffee and newspapers. One riffles idly through a pack of grimy cards. The royalty are silent, languorous as they sip their full cups. No one even glances at her. Their eyes slide past as if there were nothing to see.

The woman's head swivels and aims at the booth of factory workers. She stands quickly, gracefully, the brimming cup balanced easily in her white hand. With surprise I notice the pale bruises and pinpoint scars that seam the insides of her arms. She doesn't move like an addict.

She walks toward the men in the booth, but only when she stands over them do they notice her. A chunky, greasy-looking man with thick arms looks up.

"Looking for something, girl?" He grins at her, his fingernails rubbing against the dirty fabric of his shirt. She looks down at him in silence until he reaches out and catches her wrist, pulling her to the cracked vinyl seat beside him. She settles with the swift, lean movements of an animal. Still holding her wrist, the greasy man speaks again. "Maybe I can help you find it, hmm? You'd like that, wouldn't you?"

His friends shift uncomfortably. One says, "C'mon, Jer," but the woman turns her face to him and he trails off in midsentence, as if he forgot what he wanted to say.

The greasy man laughs. "No, no, she *likes* real men, don't you?" He drops a dark arm across her white shoulders and gives her a squeeze. She says nothing, and the greasy man bends forward.

"See, I know what they like. Julie was just like this, remember, Julie at the office?" His hand slides down from her shoulder to rest on the suede over the first curve of her breast. "Real icy, reported me for pinching her ass once. Nice ass, too. But she wanted it, I could tell, the way she watched me. So I waited for her."

His voice drops below the hard sounds of the diner, but I am sick already. His companions look queasy, but the pale woman listens silently as the man boasts. After this she seems to have found what she wants, for her tall shape curls around the man, and his dirty hand lies uncontested on her thigh. With a shiver of anger and horror, I think maybe she likes them that way — a junked-out socialite killing time until her next shoot-up with a man violent enough to get through to her deadened nerves. I shudder away from the thought, for a moment hearing only Mike's voice, "Would you just stop *fighting?*" Pain digs through my back, and I drop my head to my hands, trying not to faint. In a red-and-black haze, I hear a beautiful, dense voice beside me say, "In a moment." Icy fingers touch my shoulder, and I jerk up and around.

Her face is six inches from my own, white with the black glasses. I notice the line of her lipstick, the strange porelessness of her skin. Her lips part and she whispers, "Remember me." I want to speak to her, but the haze thickens, separating us.

When I finally clear the dizziness from my eyes, there is a cool scent in the air around me. The woman is gone, as is the man. His companions gaze after the red Corvette pulling out of the lot. I hear one say, "So that's what happened to Julie, poor kid." And another says, "I'm not calling Tammy with that shit about overtime on the line *this* time, let him explain it." They leave and Tony clears the table of their empty cups and hers, still brimming, and there is no evidence she was ever there.

I look up at a glass case behind the counter. My reflection glares back, overlaying the cut pies inside. Ropes of dirty brown hair fall past my face, past the tight lips and the half-moon bruises of sleeplessness under my eyes. My wrists show thin and pale below the shirt's wrinkled sleeves. When I stretch, the burns on my back pull. I curl my lip.

Suddenly I can no longer bear the weight of the people around me in Vic's, even though I am afraid to be alone. I walk through the glass door and out to the Buick.

After I get out of town, I meet very few cars. The hard summer moon is full, and the mountains around Phoenix glow, saguaros and chollas hurling jagged shadows across the pale, infertile earth. Grit blows in the open window and needles my sweaty skin, drying in the wind to a crust that leaves my hair like straw. Sweat itches between my shoulder blades, above my scar. I stop once, and walk out to listen to the small cracks and rustlings of the night, but through the still air I hear a car start miles away, and I run back to my own and leave quickly. The roads under me reflect with pale iridescence from the oil that has gathered there. Three o'clock, the cheap AM radio in the Buick says, and four, and four-thirty.

The sky is harsh with dawn before I drive home to sleep in my airless apartment, curtains pinned against the light.

❏

I'm dreaming about it again. Mike is standing in the main room talking, but I can't hear his voice. I know it's the same old argument about whether we should move back to L.A., where he can get his job back at the old studio. I try to explain for the last time that this project is important, that I need to do it, but he's not listening, he's still talking. He starts to yell. I know what's coming, it always happens, and I scream at him to stay away, but I can't speak. A knife is in my hands and I stab at his chest, but nothing happens. I'm thinking that this is just a dream, I should be able to stick a fucking knife into someone, and I strike harder, but the knife leaves no wounds. He's still shouting when he grabs me with his red-hot hands.

I wake up crying. The scars on my back are on fire from my sweat in the close room. A band of late-afternoon light digs through a chink in the curtain and slices across the room. After a while my breathing steadies and I stand up. Blackness edges into the corners of my eyes and I slump against the full-length mirror on the bathroom door, letting its coolness ease the remembered burn of my back. There are no nerves beneath the scars, and I feel the dead area like a hole. When I move away, I leave an oily smear the length of my body.

There is a sundress in the closet I had forgotten about. I tie a shawl over it to hide the scars.

There is a cop car at Vic's, angling across two parking places, as if to make a quick getaway. I stop the Buick precisely between the lines.

The air-conditioned cold in the diner makes my legs cramp when I open the glass door and limp to the counter. A policeman in uniform sits in the corner booth with a man in a short-sleeved shirt and chinos, surrounded by papers. They are talking to Tony, who waves at me, but remains with them. I slip under the folding divider between the counter and the diner and pull a thick mug off a green rubber rack. The big silver machine is brewing a pot, and I snatch the half-full pot from under the thin stream and pour into the chipped porcelain. Coffee drips against the heating element, hisses and smokes away. Smoke curls around me, thick fluid ropes of it. I freeze.

"What are you doing?" Hands close on my shoulder. I tear away, the coffee pot between me and the man beside me. His face is lost, his head silhouetted by the vivid sunset sky behind him. He steps forward and the fluorescent lights behind the counter shine on Tony's face. I close my eyes, listening to the drumming of my heart.

"Jesus, you crazy? That look on your face — Here, sit down." Tony slides my coffee across the counter, splashing a bit on the patterned linoleum. I stoop under the gate and sit on the cool vinyl of the stool in front of it. I touch the puddle, which is already cold.

"I'm all right."

"You sure? You look pale." He reaches out and touches my hand as it traces random circles in the spilled coffee.

"Don't touch me. I'm fine."

"You shouldn't go back of the counter. Vic'd have my ass if he caught you back there."

"You were busy."

He shrugs. "Cops. Yeah. You hear about the murders?"

He waits for me to say, gee, yes, how awful, or, no, tell me. I shrug. After a pause, he goes on.

"They found someone killed up in the hills. Third this week, a regular spree. Always their throats cut. All low-lifes, like felons and pimps and shit, sorry about the language. The guy was here last night, so they were asking around."

Sweat cools on my spine and I shiver. "Which one?"

He frowns. "Shit, I forgot you were here. They'll want to talk to you. C'mon."

I trail him to the cops at the table, balancing my cup carefully. More coffee slops over the brim and across my knuckles, and I remember the pale woman with her balanced brimming cup. The two men at the table look up at Tony curiously. The one in the chinos is skinny and dark, his hair a flat gray at the temples. The uniformed policeman is taller and has no gray.

"This is Ell. She was here last night, so I figured you'd want to talk to her."

The heads swivel to me. The gray one says, "Thank you, Mr. Henderson. Do you have a couple minutes, Miss?"

I sit down. "I have time."

"I'm Jim Oberon. This is Officer Moore. We've run into a problem and we're out getting as much information as possible. Can we ask you a few questions?"

"Sure."

Oberon asks me my name and address. I spell out my middle name, Lyne, which they always get wrong. I tell them about working at the sound studio, and give them my number there.

"You do commercials?" the one in the uniform, Moore, asks.

"Sometimes."

"I love that Jack in the Box one. You do that?"

I tell him no, so he asks a few more, and after a bit I tell him yes, I did that one, just so he gets on with it.

"Do you remember what times you were here last night?"

"I suppose two till maybe three-thirty."

Oberon digs under a pile of paper held down with a saucer half full of coffee and produces a photo that's been cut in half. A man in a tuxedo smiles at the camera. His teeth are bad. A white skirt clouds around his ankles, but is cut off abruptly at the photo's sheared edge.

"This was six years ago, but he still looked like this. A little balder. Thicker-set. Did you see him yesterday?"

"He was here last night."

"I want you to tell us what happened while he was here."

"His friends don't remember?"

"I'm asking you."

"They came in, there were four of them. He was a shit." The fabric of my sundress is grinding into the scars, and I shift my weight.

"Miss Stanfield?"

"He attacked some woman at work, he was bragging about it to her."

Oberon straightens slightly, but his question is carefully casual. "Her? The woman he attacked?"

"No. Someone else." It's hard to come up with the words to talk about her. Two boys skateboard past on the sidewalk by the streetlights and I watch them spiral for a moment.

"The woman." Oberon's voice is less patient. I wrench my thoughts back.

"She was tall. Very tall, over six feet. Albino. She had white skin and white hair, and she wore sunglasses to protect her eyes."

"What was she wearing?"

"Red."

"Can you be more specific?"

A memory is there, then suddenly escapes me. I wait for it to return, and at last I shrug. "No, I can't. It was just red. And a black belt. I can't tell you more."

"This woman, what does she do?"

I tell him about her coming in the red Corvette and sitting with the men listening, how they left together. I know I'm forgetting to tell them things, but it doesn't seem worth pursuing.

The detective leans back and rubs his eyes. His little finger is missing from the first joint, with only a shiny smoothness where it should be. "Miss — Stanfield, we've talked to a few other people who were in the diner last night. None of them said anything about a six-foot-tall albino woman who left in a Corvette. Why do you suppose that is?"

"She was there."

"Can you remember any details about this woman? What about her shoes? The license plate's state. How did she pay? Did you overhear anything?"

I frown, trying to remember the plates. "I can't remember. I didn't see her pay."

"This is all — unusual." He pauses to look at me.

"I'm not making it up."

He frowns at me a moment, then sighs and stabs at the papers with a blunt finger. "I think we have enough, Miss Stanfield. We'll have you sign a transcript of what you've told us tonight. If we have any more questions, we'll give you a ring. And if you can remember anything more about the woman, give me a call. They always know where I am at the station." He hands me a business card. I didn't know cops have business cards, and I look at it curiously. He nods in dismissal and immediately bends over the papers mounded in front of him. My legs stick to the vinyl seat as I slide out of the booth and return to the counter.

"So — what'd they ask you?" Tony's voice is low, conspiratorial. He scrubs at the counter beside me.

"Why didn't you tell them about the woman?" He looks at me blankly. "The one who left with the man they were asking about?"

"He left alone."

"I saw him leave with her. You got her coffee. Tall, white hair and skin, beautiful?"

He frowns and looks up from the spotless counter he continues to rub. "Now you mention it. Some tall white woman. But beautiful—?"

I lean forward. "But you remember her? The police say no one else does."

"I—"

The door jangles open and a young couple come in. Tony grabs two cups and a coffeepot and goes to them. When he returns, I ask, "Will you tell them?"

He looks at me for a moment. "Tell who?"

"The cops. About the pale woman. You saw her, you just said so."

"Something about a woman?..." An anxious look steals into his eyes. "I'm sorry, I can't remember what we were talking about."

"Jesus!"

He stares at me, as if I were crazy. "God, I didn't mean to upset you. We'll just forget it, all right?"

"Stop humoring me," I snap, but he's already gone, bending over the counter for another customer. I gulp the rest of my coffee, which is cold, and lay a grimy bill beside the drying puddle and the empty cup. As I leave, the two policemen, who are talking to the cook, watch me go in silence.

❏

The door slaps shut behind me, and I lean against it for a moment, trying to calm down. Sweat forms and evaporates off my body in the same instant. My scar starts to itch. I walk to my car under the glaring blue streetlights. I am fumbling with the keys when the red Corvette with the plates that say FERATA angles growling across two lanes of traffic and slides into the parking lot immediately behind me, closing me in. The driver's door opens and cold air brushes my bare legs.

She unfolds out of the driver's seat to stand beside me. It's the same red leather dress, the same black glasses utterly concealing her eyes, the same whiteness to skin and hair. I stand still, afraid to move.

"You're leaving."

I had forgotten the richness of her voice, like powder across my ears, like desert dust. I am afraid to speak, to reveal the thin scratchiness of my own voice, afraid to look at her. Instead, I look back at the diner's bright windows. Tony pours coffee for a thick man with a cigarette in a holder. The two policemen still listen to the chef, who gestures absently with a paring knife as he speaks. No one is looking out the windows at the pale woman beside me, or the Corvette pulled across the driveway's entrance.

She slouches against the hood of her car. Her neck curves away from me, half-hidden in the sheet of white hair. My eyes trace the sharp arc of her spine, softened by the furred suede that wraps it. Abruptly, she turns her head to me before I can look away. Eyes hidden by the glasses, the white face looks alien, impassive. The black lenses reflect the streetlights and the green and chrome of the diner and the dark shape that is me, distorted against the brightness.

"I'm sorry." I feel hot and awkward, caught like a child staring at someone in a wheelchair.

The red lips curl a bit, and a tiny crease shows blue by ·the corner of her mouth. "I understand."

"The man you met last night is dead."

"Is he." Her voice is neutral.

"Why are you back?"

"To find you."

"What if someone sees you?"

She gestures with one bare arm, and I am lost in the glow of her skin under the lights. Like an old film, I see her arm move through the invisibly fast flashes of the streetlamp, leaving countless impressions of itself hanging blue for an instant.

"They won't." Her voice drifts around me, deadening the street noises in my ears. I look at the red Corvette, at its gold-and-blue license plates. Still running, it growls ferally to itself.

"Is that your name — Ferata?

"It's a nickname. Tell me your name."

"Eleanor. People call me Ell." I wait for that lush voice to say something, but the silence stretches. "You're from California?"

"L.A., yes. I have contacts there."

"I know people there."

"Not my people." She smiles.

I digest this in silence, watching the people inside the diner. Still no one is looking, and I think about shouting or screaming, just to get someone, the policemen, to look up and see her. Her voice startles me, and I turn to her guiltily.

"I wanted to talk to you again. You're afraid and unhappy."

"I'm fine."

"Was it the rape?"

"I'm fine," I say again, but my voice is uncontrolled and rises too much.

"Someone once forced his will on me, though it wasn't rape. I can't forget, either."

"Will you leave me alone?" I ask half-hysterically.

"You don't have to be afraid of me."

"How can you know this stuff?"

"You were hurt, and now you're afraid of everything — other men, the world, me. But you don't have to be afraid of any of us. I've been through something like this."

"Nothing is like this."

"There are things that are worse, Eleanor."

My scars ache with the tension in my back, and I suddenly want to scream it all out at her, the whole sordid fight and the feel of his big hands throwing me over the burner. I feel my hands shaking.

She steps closer to me. I hold my ground, though I have to tilt my face back to watch stray pieces of her hair lift and drop in the slight breeze.

"You are beautiful tonight," she says. "You should always wear red."

I look down at my plain sundress and the greasy hair that falls across my face. "Bullshit."

"You are beautiful, or you will be again."

"There's nothing beautiful in me."

"Tell me what happened."

I turn away. "I can't."

Cold hands hold my shoulders. "Then cry."

I snatch myself away. "Don't touch me." Her thick voice runs around me like water, murmuring nothings. Even through the salt of my tears I smell the sweet cool scent of her. There are cold hands on my hair, but this time I don't pull away. They stroke my head and neck. I haven't been touched like that since Mike and I started fighting about our jobs. It is a touch like the night's breeze in the desert.

I lift my head. She is looking at me, the black blaze of the lens reflecting my pale face. I can't pull away.

"Don't be afraid. You've paid enough for something that wasn't your fault. You don't have to pay any more."

I nod, mesmerized by her whispering lips and her cold hands on my shoulders.

"I won't hurt you, Ell. I promise."

❏

Without the glasses, her eyes are as black as a Spaniard's. I wonder whether an albino can have such dark eyes, but only in a corner of my mind. I am drunk with the sight of her, her lush breasts and long haunches that gleam pale in the darkness of my bed. She tastes sweet and somehow familiar, like something rich and vital. Her skin stays cold, even when I run with sweat in the stifling room.

Afterwards, I lie in her arms, my fingers rubbing against the skin in the crook of her elbow. I stop on a rank of little scars.

"Why do you take drugs?"

"Drugs?" Her voice is close to my right ear. A wave of white hair falls past my face as she bends over me. My hand looks flawed, coarse and swarthy against her pale, poreless skin. She laughs her dense laugh and kisses my ear. "I don't. I have a blood deficiency. I get periodic infusions from a doctor in L.A. She thinks I am an interesting specimen."

"Are you sick?"

"No more than most people. Less than some."

"Why do the police say you don't exist?"

Again there is that thick laugh. "I exist." Her breasts catch against the sweaty scars and I flinch away from her.

"I'm sorry. It's still tender."

"Tell me about it, Eleanor." Her hands soothe the knots that rise in my neck. "Please."

"Tell you what?" I say carefully, but I know already.

"The rape."

"There's nothing to say."

"Sooner or later you'll have to talk about it, or you'll die."

I am silent for a moment. "You said you had been — it had happened to you."

"Rape, Eleanor. Say the word."

"Rape." My voice suspends itself as my throat closes. Her cool lips touch my temple and I relax again.

"I was raped," she says. "In a way. A man, he watched me dance at the saloon. They'd pay two cents a dance. But he never danced with me, he just watched. He waited for me one night, by my boardinghouse. It was over in a minute. After a while, I pulled myself together. I got him eventually, but it took a long time. He was hard to kill."

"You killed him?"

"Tell me who hurt you like this."

"You're evading my question."

"So are you." I twist around to look at her. Her black eyes gleam down, full of a complexity of emotions I can't sift through. Her white lashes sweep down — so incongruous, white against black like that — and her lips, pale with the dark lipstick gone, smile slightly. "Stop fighting. Tell me about it."

Involuntarily, I glance toward the other room. I see Mike standing in the doorway to the yard, the night behind him glowing pink with the sodium-vapor streetlight on the corner. I shiver.

"You knew him, didn't you? He was a friend."

I nod.

"And he did this to you, burned your pretty back and scarred your soul." Her voice deepens. "What happened?"

I remember fighting with Mike about work, and his wanting us to return to L.A., Mike in the doorway with the key I forgot to get back, of course I was coming back, Ell, we have to decide this, why is your job so fucking important all the time? Why won't you, it would mean so much to me, pull us together again, you always want it, will you stop fighting? And his weight pressing me over the burner he doesn't know is hot, the bitter smoke of my skin and the pain and the pain and the pain.

"It wasn't your fault, Eleanor. Do you know that yet?"

The tears drop from my face to trace silver tracks across her skin. "I could have talked to him, instead of packing his shit and throwing him out. I could have made him understand."

"But he did it. You can't change that. It wasn't your fault. He hurt you."

I start to cry in earnest. The sobs are like dry heaves, wrenching my bones with their violence. "Goddammit. God damn him."

"What was his name?"

"Mike Prini."

Cold hands stroke the tears from my face until it is over. At last I open my eyes.

"How do you know?" I ask, exhausted.

"I sense general things, emotions."

"Like ESP?"

She smiles tightly. "No, like an animal."

I pull at a strand of my hair that has fallen across my face. It clings to my finger in a perfect curl. "How did you make it?"

"Time took the worst away, but I still have his scars." She gestures enigmatically at her white face.

"But you're beautiful."

She shifts restlessly under me, pulls free of my sticky skin. "It's four already. I have to eat."

"I have stuff."

"Not like that."

"You'd leave me?" I struggle upright, tangled in the sweaty sheets. She slides the red dress over her head; it falls and clings as if used to the curves of her body.

"I'll see you again," she says.

"But it's still dark."

"Don't worry."

I nod, but the fear tears at my chest.

Her eyes full of compassion, she leans over to kiss me. Her lips against mine, she whispers, "You have nothing to be afraid of. It was not the night that hurt you."

❏

The doorbell. I roll over into an empty pillow, but it rings on. At last I stagger upright and weave to the door. Squinting through the peephole, I see a man in a suit and another in black. The sun behind them, half-hidden under great gathering clouds, makes an aureole of their hair. I recognize the man in the suit as Oberon. I am suddenly wide awake.

"Yes?" I ask through the door.

"Eleanor Stanfield?"

"What is it?"

In synchronous motion they pull identical billfolds from their pockets, and flip them open to show to the peephole. I catch the glint of badges. "Detective Oberon, Officer Moore. I talked to you yesterday. May we come in?"

I pull on the red dress that lays in a heap on the floor, unlatch the door, and let it fall open. "What is it?"

"It's about a former co-worker of yours, a Michael Prini. This afternoon he was found dead. I'm afraid it's the same as the others."

"*What?*"

"You filed charges a few months ago against Mr. Prini. We'd like you to come down to the station and answer a few questions."

"Mike's dead?"

I stumble out the door.

❑

My eyelids hurt from squinting against the bright room. Overchilled air beats my body into a dull ache. They pound questions at me. What about the rape? How had I felt about it? Where had I been last night, with whom, alone? No, they weren't accusing me of anything, they were just checking. I tell them what I can, but things keep jumping away, I keep forgetting. A styrofoam cup of coffee is in my hand: it is cold, so it must have been there for some time. Oberon hands me another card. If I think of anything...

It is dark and raining hard cold pellets when they take me back to where the Buick sits, slick with rain, on the asphalt by my home. My wet windshield slurs with street light as I pull onto Valdez. A car honks, then another. It takes a moment to realize they are honking at me, and another to realize why: I pull a knob and my headlights flash on.

The streets run with water like black rivers. Damp with rain, my dress sticks to the car seat. I can feel her skin under my fingers as I grip the cold, slick steering wheel. Her scent is caught in my hair, freed when I shake it back from my face.

I drive four times down Central before I find what I am looking for. In front of a small bar struggling under the weight of its neon crouches the red Corvette with plates that say FERATA.

It is hard to find her in the dark bar. She sits alone in a back booth, where the red bulbs in their absurd ships' lanterns turn her skin and her dress the same carmine color. She glows against the burgundy leather of the banquette, except for her black eyes.

I can't see anything but the glow of her. Blinded by the neon, I stumble through the dark room, and I slam into a black shape. My hands shoot out, but the shape tilts and overturns. There is a crash and hot clear pain crosses my palm. Someone curses as I step through the mess and walk on.

"You hurt yourself. You'd better sit down." Her voice is just as I remembered it, thick and concerned. Blood from my cut hand drips pale in the red light, falls like oil from my fingertips to vanish in the dark air.

"I won't sit with you."

A waiter kneels by the fallen table, picking broken glass from the carpet. An older couple stands by the pile of glass and china, their voices loud with anger. No one is looking at me.

"What is it you do to them? No one ever sees me when I'm with you."

"It's me they don't see. You're hurt. Please sit down." Her cold hand touches my injured wrist. I think of the blood dropping from my fingers and snatch my hand from her. She smiles bitterly. "Never from you, Eleanor. Unless you wished it. And then gladly."

Unable to stand, I drop to the cool leather across from her, sobbing.

"Why do you do it?"

She sits, a bloody alabaster statue in the bloody light. "If I have to kill, I'd prefer they deserved it."

"*Mike?*"

"He raped you."

"We lived together. He took me to visit his mother in Colorado once. He was just a guy." It is very cold in the bar. I huddle down into the leather.

She bends her head over the untouched glass sweating before her. "I have to live, Eleanor. The doctor cannot give me everything I need."

"The police think I did it."

"They'll forget."

"You used me to find him and now he's dead."

She reaches across the table and touches my face. "Eleanor, I didn't use you. I couldn't. You're too beautiful to me, even scarred." She brushes tears from my cheeks. "So small a thing to miss, tears." Her hand drops, then raises to push back the hair that has fallen across her face. I shiver with the remembrance of that hair against my skin. Her eyes are black below the red-lit fingers.

"I used to have black hair, like my Spanish mother's." She strokes her throat absently. "I wanted to cry when I saw it leach white, and my skin, but there were no tears in these eyes. They only burned, as they burned for the first one that died, and the second. After a while, they stopped burning." She laughs, but her mouth is twisted. "Such a small thing to miss. But he never asked. He didn't even care. A hundred years, and I still won't forgive him.

"You will heal, Eleanor, and walk bare-backed in the sun. And I — I will kill again," she says with another little laugh, "but I will know what I killed."

She stands with graceful speed. She leans over and kisses me, her lips soft against mine, and straightens. And she is gone.

❏

I come home in the darkness. I flick the light switch beside the door, but it flares and dies. I stumble through the shadows to my unmade bed, to sleep.

The sheets are kicked into a pile on the floor when I awake in my hot, dark room. I am sheathed in my own sweat, but above its bite there is a scent, sweet and familiar, that hurts me even as I smile. The new scab on my hand pulls as I stretch across the bed to unpin the curtains. I am clumsy, but at last the silver pins fall to the floor and the latch is opened, and August sun and morning breeze fills my windows. As I stand, my bare foot nudges something cool and light under the bed. I grope in the dust and my fingers close on a slim, curved wand — an ear piece. Wraparound sunglasses with lenses like night. I dress and walk out alone into the sun, night-colored glasses folded tight in my hand.

The Strawberry Man
John Peyton Cooke

Tenny and André were cruising along the sidewalk on their skateboards when they caught sight of the old man. Tenny had been staring so intently at André's ass twisting and turning ahead of him that he might never have noticed the man, if it hadn't been for the shiny aluminum hardhat he was wearing. The old man was dressed in work clothes selling strawberries, the sun's bright reflection beaming from his silvery hat, right into Tenny's eyes.

"Hey, André!" Tenny shouted, bringing himself to a halt near the entrance of a gravel road. "Hold up." Tenny flipped his skateboard up under his arm; it was carved all over with the names of his favorite bands.

André stopped and asked, "What for, man?" He bent over to pick up his skateboard, his cut-off sweatpants riding up the cleft of his ass cheeks.

The sun shone brilliantly through an open patch of blue, but was about to be enveloped by the low-hanging, dark storm clouds that covered most of the sky. Tenny and André both dripped with sweat, their shorts and t-shirts clinging to their skin from the oppressive mugginess of the afternoon. They were out of breath, and thirsty.

The gravel road stretched into the woods and over the hill, to the strawberry fields, where anyone could go pick their own fresh for a small fee.

"Look," said Tenny, pointing at the man.

Two ancient oak trees were stationed on either side of the gravel road, providing ample shade. Yet the man had parked his pickup truck out away from the trees, closer to the sidewalk, and was sitting on the open tailgate in the direct sunlight, where he sorted out piles of freshly picked strawberries and put them in green, quart-sized containers. His plump figure entirely filled the large pair of overalls that he wore over a white short-sleeved t-shirt. The dark sunglasses sitting on his pudgy, sunburnt face hid his eyes completely from view. The hardhat he wore on his head looked incredibly uncomfortable in the damp heat. As he worked, he ate his own strawberries noisily, his fat double chin bobbing up and down as he chewed.

"Howdy, boys," said the man with a grin. His aging teeth displayed a pinkish tint.

Now he was twenty-one, Tenny no longer appreciated being called a boy, but he supposed his spiked hair and ragged t-shirt, André's mohawk and multiple earrings, as well as their skateboards, made them both seem immature to this old guy.

"Here, boys, free samples," said the man, and handed them two apiece. "Freshest strawberries you'll ever eat."

Tenny looked at the strawberries piled up in the bed of the pickup, and examined the two in his hand more closely. They were perfect in every respect, a bright glossy red, over two inches long, their round tapered shape as balanced as a top, and capped with a small leafy crown and a slightly curved stem. They were prime examples of strawberries, good enough for an advertisement, and certainly good enough to eat.

Tenny held his strawberries up to André's face. "Just look at them. They're beautiful!"

Tenny bit into one. The sweet, tangy flavor flooded his taste buds with delight. André started nibbling his.

"Looks like rain, I'd say," said the old man.

"Mmm. Delicious," said Tenny. He bought a whole quart, promising André he would share them with him.

The sun disappeared behind a cloud, and a low rumbling could be heard in the distance. The air smelled like rain. It could start to pour any minute, Tenny figured.

"Thanks, guy," said Tenny to the old man.

The man's cheery red face smiled back a them. "No, thank you. Bye now, fellas. Come on back."

"Sure," said André. Then to Tenny: "Give me a few of those."

"Come on, let's get back to the apartment. It's going to soak us in a few seconds." They hopped on their skateboards and started off. Tenny carried the quart of strawberries with his left hand, tucking it under his arm.

A flash of lightning lit up the gray sky, followed soon after by an earth-shattering crack of thunder.

Tenny glanced back over his shoulder, and saw the man was gone. He did a double take. The man must have wanted to beat the rain, but he couldn't possibly have gotten away so quickly.

"Hey, watch it!"

Tenny looked ahead just in time to find himself running smack into André. They fell off their boards and landed together on the grass in a heap. Tenny's face ended up in André's armpit, where he got a good whiff of his musk, while his thigh landed in André's crotch, nearly racking him. The strawberries went flying, most of them landing in the gutter or the street.

"Get off of me, you slut," said André.

Tenny got up and grabbed his skateboard from nearby, where it had struck a chain-link fence. A car zoomed by, squishing several strawberries beneath its tires.

It started to rain.

"Fucking hell," said Tenny.

❏

It was raining again the next day by the time Tenny woke up. He put a Revolting Cocks disc in the CD player, opened a can of Meister Brau for himself, and sat down with the *Chicago Sun-Times*. André came out from the bedroom naked, scratching the stubbly scalp beneath his mohawk and yawning. "Morning," he stated.

"Afternoon," said Tenny, grinning at André slyly.

"Shit."

"Stud."

"Slut." André's eyes were bleary, but he looked good. His upper body was solidly built, and he had taut, well-muscled drummer's arms. He was part of a band called Mach Twang that played industrial dance music verging on speedmetal, and he channeled all of his energy into his drumming. There wasn't an ounce of fat on his body, since it was all sweated off in their rehearsals and occasional gigs. Whatever energy he had left over Tenny received in the form of a hard cock up his butt.

"Let's see if that strawberry guy is out again today," said André, opening his beer.

"You read my mind," said Tenny. André often did, they had known each other so long. "Oh, you got some mail. Your student loan went through." Tenny handed him the letter from the bank.

"Cooler than shit! Not a word to my folks."

"Nada." Tenny couldn't tell André's parents because André wasn't going to return to school come September. Instead, he was going to put most of the money in the band fund. Any money Mach Twang was making now was negligible; on some gigs they made money, on some they lost, and it turned out even. Yet they had expenses to cover — renting the PA, paying the sound company, not to mention transportation. They needed money, and all the band members were pitching in. André was going to contribute his student loan. He only hoped the band could land a contract with Wax Trax or some other independent label before his parents found out he had dropped out of school. Luckily, they lived a thousand miles away and wouldn't know any better.

"We'll just have to celebrate," said André. "Let's go get some strawberries."

They went on their skateboards, through the pelting rain, to the entrance of the gravel road where the old man had been the day before. But there was nothing there except the two old oak trees, their leaves fluttering in the wind and rain. It rained all day long, and the man selling strawberries was nowhere to be found.

❏

The rain cleared up the following morning, and by noon with the sun out the temperature had reached ninety-one degrees, with 74-percent humidity, according to the clerk at the 7-Eleven, where Tenny had gone to buy beer.

They found the man where he had been before, sitting on the tailgate of his pickup truck in the bright sun. His red face greeted them with a smile, his hardhat and sunglasses reflecting the sun into their eyes.

"How did you like 'em, boys?" asked the man.

Tenny laughed, embarrassed. "We didn't get to eat any. I accidentally tossed them in the street. That's why we're back."

"Well, I daresay I got myself a better batch today, anyhow. They've been sitting here just waiting for some good folk like yourselves to come along and—"

"I'm Tenny, and this is André," he said, offering his hand. The old man shook hands with him, leaving Tenny's pink and sticky and smelling of strawberries.

André shook hands with him, too, but seemed impatient. "We'll take two quarts this time. We only want your best."

"Got 'em right here." The man showed them two quarts of freshly picked strawberries like none they had ever seen. Each strawberry was perfect in shape, color, texture, smell, as if hand-crafted by gods. Tenny and André each grabbed a quart for themselves. André handed the man some bills, and the man gave him his change.

"You out here every day?" asked André, setting down his skateboard and placing one foot upon it.

"Whenever the sun shines and the sky is blue, yessir. For one more week, then I move on."

Tenny hopped on his skateboard and asked, "You got a name, guy?"

The man popped a strawberry in his mouth and began to chew. "Oh, I'm just the Strawberry Man," he said. "It was nice making your acquaintance."

Tenny and André looked at each other puzzledly, and Tenny shrugged and said, "Okay."

"C'mon, slut, let's blow."

They blew.

❏

They dumped the strawberries together in a large bowl, and set them on the kitchen table.

"Wow!" said André. "Look at them."

"Incredible," muttered Tenny, mostly to himself. "Go ahead."

André hesitated, then reached for the topmost strawberry and quickly devoured it. "Your turn."

Tenny took one and stared at it for a moment, looking for a flaw — a bruise, a nick, a discoloration, anything. But there was none. He couldn't resist any longer, and promptly ate it. It was the most divine taste he had ever encountered.

From that point on, it was almost a race. Tenny and André sat down and munched strawberries one after the other, like two chain smokers getting their nicotine fix. They made grunts and groans of pleasure, licked their fingers like little boys, and barely allowed any time to savor the flavor of one strawberry before putting the next in their mouths. Tenny's heart beat faster with excitement as the bowl become further depleted. His taste buds were so satisfied, he was even getting an erection. Tenny wondered if perhaps he had found a legitimate aphrodisiac, but quickly realized that idea was mistaken; he felt like making love, yes, but not to André — to a *strawberry*.

Suddenly, a car horn blared loudly outside.

"Oh, shit!" said André, looking at his watch. "It's three o'clock. I'm supposed to take some ad copy down to the newspaper for our gig tomorrow night, and do some postering. Rick's going to take me into the city. I've got to go."

"You'll be a few hours or so?"

"Yeah," said André, grabbing a manila folder from beside the phone. He took a handful of strawberries, looked suspiciously at Tenny, gave him a kiss, and added, "Save half of those for me or you die."

❑

After first putting on a Ministry CD and cranking the sound, Tenny moved the bowl of strawberries to the coffee table in the living room and shoved the alternative music magazines and assorted independent rags to the floor. Then he sorted the berries into two piles, separate but equal.

He decided he would only eat from his own pile, and leave the others for André, his fair share after all. He chewed sweet, juicy chunks of strawberry flesh, and his senses tingled. With his eyes closed, he couldn't help but sit there grinning stupidly while the juicy nectar slid down his throat. He was in heaven.

Before long, he was down to his last strawberry. He held it between thumb and forefinger and considered it, rolling it back and forth. He bit the tip off it, and glanced nervously at the coffee table. André's considerable pile of strawberries sat there, tempting him.

But he was determined not to eat André's strawberries. He would have to make the most of what he had.

Where he had already taken a bite, Tenny smeared the strawberry across his lips, an electric sensation along the sensitive, chapped skin. Tenny hopped to his feet, went into the bathroom, and stood before the mirror. A glossy pinkish stain coated his mouth. He took the strawberry and rubbed it on the skin beneath his cheekbones, and turned his head so he could see a three-quarter view of himself. *Damn, he looked good!* He rubbed the strawberry across his eyelids. *Perfect.* He put a pink streak in his blond, spiked hair. *Too fucking cool.* He threw off his t-shirt and pressed the strawberry against one nipple, then the other. This was too much; he was getting an erection again. He squeezed the strawberry and let a pink trickle of juice flow down his chest. Then, finally, he couldn't resist any longer, and ate it.

André's return was still an hour or two away.

Tenny went back to the living room. There was no way he could hold out until André got back. The pile sat waiting in the bowl, a brilliant red treasure upon the dull, dusty coffee table.

"Methinks thou dost mock me," said Tenny aloud, irreverently, before sitting down and eating them.

❏

Tenny was drunk when André entered the apartment. Crushed cans of Meister Brau were strewn about, and the old, scratched Killing Joke CD he had just put on was skipping, arbitrarily spitting out snatches of primal drum beats at random to Tenny's pleasure and amusement. From his seat on the couch, Tenny smiled at André and offered him the last of his beer, clutched shakily in his hand.

André looked at the empty bowl on the coffee table and frantically glanced in the kitchen. Tenny half expected to see steam purging from his ears, then laughed uncontrollably at the thought.

"Where are my strawberries?" demanded André.

Tenny pointed to his own mouth. "Sorry, stud, I couldn't help it. They were too good."

André's face was rigid. He rushed over to the couch and looked intently at Tenny's face. Then, suddenly André kissed him firmly on the lips, poking his tongue into Tenny's mouth and swirling it around, exploring every corner. Tenny was too stunned, as well as too drunk, to think. André had looked more like he was about to hit him than kiss him. But at last, André broke the kiss, scowling.

"Damn," he said. "All I can taste is beer."

"So what?"

"I don't give a shit about turning you on. I'm just looking for some strawberry."

❏

Above the entrance to the ancient, soot-blackened brick warehouse, the sign read:

THE OVENS
entre at yr owne ryske

in blue and pink neon. Green photocopied posters advertising tonight's show, with ("Chicago's own") Baby Spiders opening up for ("suburban snots") Mach Twang, were plastered outside the entrance beneath two bright, bare light bulbs. Tenny stumbled up the crumbling cement steps to the door, and smirked at the bouncer. He didn't have to tell the guy he was on the guest list for Mach Twang. He was known here, and was never any trouble. Even though he didn't need to have his hand stamped, he asked to have it done anyway, because he like to have proof that he was a nifty guy.

Tenny had felt moody, depressed, and shaky ever since the previous evening, after he had eaten the last of the strawberries. At least being drunk had helped. But now that he was dry, with a hangover to boot, he felt like shit. Purple, puffy bags hung beneath his eyes, and his muscles were tied up in knots. His mind was all goofy; he couldn't tell if the stamp on his hand was a dragon's head or the letter G.

Baby Spiders were already thrashing away on stage, and a small group of people were slam-dancing all over the floor. Many were wearing severely distressed pairs of jeans, with white t-shirts and leather jackets. The bodies bounced off one another in an ecstatic blur. But there weren't yet enough people out there for it to be any fun.

The smoke-filled interior of the Ovens was done in black and white, with café-style iron tables and chairs circling the floor in two terraced levels surrounding the stage. The gray walls were lit with subdued lights of varied color shooting upwards from the floor. Plastic plants throughout were spray-painted an ashen tone. Poseurs, punks, a few hippies and rastafarians, and other assorted types crowded around the tables everywhere, talking and smoking while they avidly downed their drinks.

Tenny went to the bar and bought a Rolling Rock. He took a large gulp, his hand shaking uncontrollably. He was eager to get drunk, to rid himself of this desperate craving for the old man's strawberries. He hadn't been able to eat all day, because his stomach wouldn't take anything else; the hot dog he had eaten at lunch had immediately come right back out. He could recall how the strawberries had tasted, but this only made it worse, and did nothing to satisfy his desire.

Tenny stepped out in between bands for a breath of fresh air. By this time, the Oven had filled up and was teeming with warm, sweaty bodies. He sat on the steps smoking a cigarette, and he couldn't believe his eyes when he saw, parked in the shadows on the other side of the street, the pickup truck belonging to the Strawberry Man.

He dashed across the street, absently letting his cigarette fall from his lips. The pickup smelled wonderful, but there were no strawberries in either the bed or the cab; all he could see through the grimy windows were red stains on the white vinyl bench seat. In any case, the truck was locked. Tenny glanced around anxiously, looking up and down the street, but saw no sign of the Strawberry Man.

André must have invited him to the gig.

Taking one last whiff of the strawberry-mobile, Tenny grinned with anticipation and raced back into the club.

Mach Twang's gear was all set up on the stage, so it was clear they were about to go on. Bessie, one of the waitresses, was going about from table to table, setting aluminum pie plates at each one; they were filled with strawberries.

"Courtesy of Mach Twang," the girl intoned at every stop. "Courtesy of Mach Twa—"

Tenny grabbed a handful out of the tin she was holding.

"Go ahead, Tenny," she said. "They're free."

"Fucking incredible," he said, popping two in his mouth. "Where'd you get them?"

"Your friends—" said Bessie, munching on a strawberry. "'Scuse me. Your friends brought them. They're in the dungeon."

Finishing his wad of strawberries, Tenny pushed through the crowd and opened the door near the stage that led to the basement. He rushed down the steep, rickety stairs, tripping down the last two steps, the result of too many beers.

"Ain't it cool, Tenny? Ain't it?" André leapt from his seat on a box of wine coolers when he saw Tenny. He grabbed several strawberries from a nearby tin and started feeding them to Tenny, shoving them one by one into his mouth. Gene, Travis, and Fred, the rest of Mach Twang, laughed while they stood around eating. Their faces were stark and shadowy in the harsh light of the single hanging bulb.

"Mmmph!" Tenny tried to speak. "Gmmgmmph." He put his hands up and waved frantically to get André to stop stuffing berries down his throat.

"Sorry, Tenny."

Tenny chewed them up and swallowed them in a few big gulps. "Jeez, how'd you get so many?'

"I bought them." André kissed him, both of their lips sticky with strawberry juice, their tongues slippery sweet.

Of course, with his loan André had beaucoup bucks.

"I saw the Strawberry Man's truck—" Tenny looked about the room, which was nothing more than a supply room, small and damp, with stone walls, filled with boxes of booze. At this club, it was the only private place a band could have to themselves before going on stage. Atop the stacks of boxes, everywhere, were more plates of strawberries than Tenny could count. "So where is he?"

André motioned drunkenly at the closed door on the opposite wall. "In there, that little room. He stashed his strawberries there when he came." A sign on the door said: *Do Not Disturb.*

"I didn't see him come in the club," said Tenny.

"Neither did we," said Fred. "He was here when we came down, after Baby Spiders was done."

The door opened a crack, and the Strawberry Man's arm set a new, full pan alongside several others on a case of beer. Then the door slammed shut.

"Guys," said Gene, "we gotta go. C'mon. Travis, got the song list?"

"Mmmph," said Travis.

"Here," said André, handing Tenny his own personal plate of strawberries. "Enjoy. See you after."

Tenny popped a berry into his mouth. After the band had left the dungeon, he thought of opening the door across the room and saying hello to the Strawberry Man, but something held him back. He turned and bounded up the stairs, being careful not to spill his plate.

◻

By the time Mach Twang had finished their seventh song, everybody in the Ovens was munching on strawberries. The pie plates were all over, on tables, bannisters, bar stools, and at the edge of the stage; there was plenty. Grinning teeth glistened through the dim light. Self-absorbed mods were licking sticky juice off their fingers, while pretty poseurs licked each other's. Even the punks were emerging from the pool of jerking limbs and thrashing mohawks every so often to grab more handfuls of strawberries, which they put in their jacket pockets and ate while they slammed.

Tenny ate quickly, listening to the deafening roar of distortion. The machine-gun rapid pounding and beating of André's drums penetrated his body as deeply as did André's prick when they were in bed. He wanted desperately to plunge into the crowd and join the slam-dancing. But he couldn't until his plate was finished.

The band was playing one of the first songs they had written, "Mary Mace":

My mom was CIA Mary Mace
Never let go of her leatherette briefcase...

Something was wrong.

Tenny looked all around the club, at the hundreds of people eating strawberries. He wondered what the hell was so special about these things, why they were so delicious, and why it was impossible to stop eating them or, after tasting them, to eat anything else. They were not ordinary. Something was definitely wrong.

Fred, the singer and guitarist, announced into the microphone, "We just wrote this: 'Discombobulated.'" The band let loose right away. The beat was fast, furious, ideal for slam-dancing. The guitars cut a jagged rhythm, while Travis's slick synthesizer tracks wailed high above in a frenzied intro. Gene's throbbing bass and André's frenetic drumming meshed together, sounding like an old heavy-duty washing machine in the spin cycle.

Nervous, little, agitated
Now you're incarcerated...

Tenny was down to a handful of strawberries. He twisted the pie plate into a ball and threw it at Fred's head: it bounced off Fred's ear and landed on the stage. Tenny held tightly onto the last of his berries and went out onto the dance floor. He pushed his way through the leather, denim, pale skin, haircuts, and sideburns until he was where the action was. Then it was out of control. He was shoving, being pushed and punched, throwing his clenched fists around, banging up against countless bodies...

Feeble and frustrated
They want you eradicated...

He popped some strawberries into his mouth. Someone slammed up against him, forcing him to bite his tongue. He could taste the blood swirling in his mouth with the strawberry juice. He spat. The watery pink mixture hit the nape of a skinhead's neck, just below his swastika tattoo, and then suddenly three or four bodies thrust into the space between Tenny and the skinhead, before the skinhead disappeared into the crowd, just another pretty face, gone forever. Tenny was being spun around, letting the crowd dictate his movements. He was shoved up against the stage, his rib cage squeezed in by a mass of punks, and then the pressure was gone, and he was flying back into the swirl of arms and poking elbows. He shoved against a couple guys, then slipped on the beer-slick floor, but was quickly helped back up by nine reaching, grabbing arms. The last of his strawberries were scattered on the floor; people were picking them up, some getting their fingers stomped on, but they didn't seem to care. They gobbled them up, smiling...

Thank Pigs Incorporated...

"Hey! Goddammit!" Tenny shouted, but of course no one heard him above the music. He caught a glimpse of Bessie's face going past in a blur. "Hey!" he thrust his way through and grabbed her shoulder. She spun around. He dragged her out of the storm, to the outer fringes, and shouted into her ear, "You got any more?"

"What?"

"You got any more strawberries?"

"No! You?"

You're discombobulated
Brain has evaporated...

"Wait, there's some." Tenny rushed up to one of the cafe tables, around which sat several rastafarians finishing off a plate of strawberries. He sneaked his hand in and grabbed a few.

"Hey, mon!" one of them cried.

Tenny ignored him. Bessie came up and said, "C'mon, Tenny, where's mine?"

He gave her a sneer and said, "Piss off." Right away, he devoured the rest.

Gonna be eviscerated
Mangled and emasculated...

The club was sweltering. Sweat was flowing as profusely as the beer, and by now most people had stripped down to their soaked t-shirts. People all around Tenny were going from table to table, looking for more strawberries. There were still a few to be had, but the people who had them were uninterested in sharing.

Tenny's stomach rumbled. A strawberry-flavored belch erupted from his throat. He had to have more.

Thank Pigs Incorporated
Pigs Incorporated
Pigs Incorporated
Pigs Incorporated...

Tenny's mouth went dry, and his limbs shook.

When the song was finished and the cheering died down, Fred said into the microphone the band would be taking a short break before starting their second set. Tenny pushed his way through the crowd, to the stage, to catch André before he went down into the dungeon. He grabbed André's arm.

"Tenny! We're a hit tonight, huh? Won't be long till Wax Trax picks us up. What do you think?"

"Hey, stud, are there any more strawberries?"

"Yeah, yeah, don't worry. The man says he has an endless stash. There'll be more coming up for the second set."

"Good deal. How much did this cost you?"

"All of it."

"Are you crazy?"

"Hey, I did it for you, slut. I mean, I knew how much you liked them and stuff, and I wanted some more, too. I thought it would be wild to turn the crowd onto them—"

"But I can't stop eating them. Nobody can. Something's wrong."

"Yeah, sure, I know. I was screwing up all over the place, I had the shakes so bad. I munched a few in between songs, but not enough. Not nearly enough. What, do you think they're laced with LSD or something?"

"How the fuck should I know?"

"Well, what do you want me to do about it?"

"Just get me some more. I think I'm going to pass out or something."

"Sure. We'll be back up in a sec. Sit tight." Then André was gone down the staircase, into the depths.

A tape was now playing over the PA, yet Tenny could hear the crowd's commotion rumbling beneath. No more strawberries were left, and people were getting anxious. It wouldn't be much longer until someone in the club started getting violent.

Maybe it'll be me, Tenny thought as he punched his palm with his fist. He was beginning to get a headache. His mouth was dry, but he knew he wouldn't be able to drink another beer. His stomach knew what it wanted.

They all waited. Most of them smoked one cigarette after another, ignoring their friends and staring into the swirling haze of smoke and damp air. Tenny paced around the club peeking into every corner and eyeing everyone with apprehension. The poseurs were snottier than usual, the punks were growing more paranoid and obnoxious, while the few hippies looked simply stunned. The only people the slightest amiable were some of the rastafarians sitting around a table, eagerly discussing their plans for drying some of the strawberries and smoking them, once they got hold of more.

Sparse applause greeted Mach Twang when they got on stage and started fiddling with their instruments. Fred tuned his guitar and came up to the microphone. "Hi," he said. "There'll be more strawberries coming up."

The crowd whooped and hollered.

Someone shouted, "When?"

"They're coming, so just hang on a minute! Travis wrote this one: 'Enema of the State.'"

The band started playing, but they weren't playing very well, and no one seemed to care one way or the other. The people on the floor were just milling about nervously, uninterested in slam-dancing. Few people paid any attention to the band. Tenny noticed they kept losing the beat, perhaps distracted by what was going on in the club, or perhaps because they needed more strawberries themselves.

The crowd started booing and hissing, and then it rose into a huge uproar.

"Fuck you!" shouted one woman, over and over. "Fuck you, Mach Twang! Fuck you!"

The band members looked anxiously at each other, confused and angry. They faltered. Gene lost the bass line entirely, and when he reentered, he was off a few beats. André's drumming wasn't steady, Fred kept hitting wrong chords, and all of this clashed with Travis's mostly preprogrammed synthesizer tracks.

"More strawberries!" someone yelled. Then, everyone was up on the floor, crowding in close to the stage, their fists raised. Many were still booing. A few were locked in small scuffles with one another, getting bruised and battered. They all demanded more.

Tenny was still shaking when he saw the Strawberry Man appear from out of the dungeon. No one else seemed to notice him, their attention focused on the stage — but then none of them knew who he was, anyway. He was dressed exactly as he had been the other times Tenny had seen him, and he was smiling.

Two punks rushed up onto the stage, heading for Fred. Just as they did, the band stopped playing, and André stood up from behind the drums and shouted into his own microphone, "Stop!" He pointed at the Strawberry Man. "Look over there, that's the guy who brought the strawberries. If you want more, talk to him! We're fucking through with this shit!"

André, Fred, Gene, and Travis walked off the stage and were enveloped by the closely packed crowd. Tenny was so eager for more strawberries that he paid no attention to where André was — he didn't really give a shit.

All eyes shifted to look at the Strawberry Man as his rotund figure climbed up the steps, onto the stage. Much commotion arose from all around the club, but when the Strawberry Man stood at the center and looked out over the people, they all abruptly went quiet. He grabbed Fred's microphone from its stand and held it in his flabby fingers.

Feedback squawked before he began. "So, you like my strawberries?" he asked.

The crowd cheered, and some shouted, "More!" as they would have done to get the band to do an encore.

"Oh, there's plenty more where the first batch came from, believe me. And you're welcome to all you can eat. André was quite generous with his money."

Everyone broke out into cheers and applause, waving approving fists in the air.

"Children," the Strawberry Man said, his voice sounding like thunder over the powerful PA system, "I think the second batch is ready now."

Tenny watched closely as the Strawberry Man removed his sunglasses. Behind the pale eyelids, where his eyeballs should have been, there were instead two ripe strawberries, bright red and glistening. He laughed through his rotting, pink teeth, grinning like a madman. Then he removed his hardhat. Beneath, he was missing his skull cap, and his brain was replaced by a pile of fat, juicy strawberries. As they started spilling out, Tenny thought they looked even more perfect than the ones he had devoured so rapturously the night before. The Strawberry Man bent over, as if taking a bow, and strawberries began streaming out the top of his head in a seemingly endless flow, cascading over the people and onto the floor.

The crowd scrambled after them.

Tenny shoved his way through the chaos to the center, and ate every strawberry he could get his hands on. They were fantastic.

The Strawberry Man kept on laughing.

About the contributors

John Peyton Cooke is the author of the gay vampire novel *Out for Blood* (Avon, 1991), as well as the gay-themed horror novel *The Lake* (Avon, 1989). His short fiction has appeared in *Weird Tales*. He was born in 1967 in Amarillo, Texas, and grew up in Laramie, Wyoming. He now lives in Madison, Wisconsin, where he works as a stenographer for the Madison Police Department.

Jewelle Gomez is a writer and activist in New York City. She is the author of *Flamingoes and Bears*, a collection of poetry. *The Gilda Stories* (Firebrand, 1991) is her first novel.

Kij Johnson started writing fiction in 1985. She attended the 1987 Clarion West Writers' Workshop in Seattle. Her fiction has appeared in *Amazing, Weird Tales, Pulphouse,* and *Twilight Zone Magazine*. She lives in New York and is at work on a novel. "Ferata" was first published in *Pulphouse* 1 (1988).

Nina Kiriki Hoffman is one of seven mutant children. Her mother was an actress and is a peace activist, and her father once belonged to a think tank and now works with computers. Her siblings are art-workers too, mostly in music and movies. Hoffman's short fiction has appeared in *Asimov's, Hitchcock's, Weird Tales, Pulphouse, Amazing Stories,* and a variety of horror anthologies. She has tales forthcoming in *Aboriginal SF* and *Analog.*

Hubert Kennedy is the author of *Ulrichs: Karl Heinrich Ulrichs, Pioneer of the Modern Gay Movement* (Alyson, 1988) and the translator of two gay novels by the Scotch-German anarchist and boy lover John Henry Mackay: *The Hustler* (Alyson, 1985) and *Fenny Skaller* (1988).

Jay B. Laws has published dozens of short stories in a variety of local and national magazines, including the *New York Native, Advocate Men, This Week in Texas,* and the *Castro Times.* He is also a playwright, with plays produced on New York, Los Angeles, and San Francisco stages. His supernatural horror novel *Steam* (Alyson, 1991) won A Different Light Bookstore's grand prize for best new novel. He is currently at work on a collection of ghost stories called *Stories for the Unfinished,* and lives in San Francisco.

Jeffrey N. McMahan, a resident of Los Angeles, is the author of *Somewhere in the Night,* the 1989 Lambda Literary Award winner for Gay Men's Science Fiction/Fantasy, and *Vampires Anonymous,* a novel about Andrew the Vampire, both from Alyson. He is a member of the Los Angeles Gay and Lesbian Writers Circle and the Third Street Writers Group.

Adrian Nikolas Phoenix has had stories published in *Amazing Stories, Pulphouse,* and various small press publications. She works as a clerk in a science fiction bookstore in Eugene, Oregon, and as a typesetter for a local specialty press. She does horror readings at SF/fantasy/

horror conventions, often previewing her work before her best critics — her sons. She is currently working on half a dozen different projects and, not so quietly, going crazy. "Sacrament" first appeared in *Amazing Stories*, January 1990.

Peter Robins's collection *Undo Your Raincoats and Laugh* (Red Robin, 1977) was the first book of openly gay short stories to appear in England. Since then he has produced three other collections. His most recent play, *Ricks*, has been produced in London and Paris. The latest of his four novels, *Stony Glances*, was published in February 1991. He lives in London and is a partner in Third House Publishers.

D.T. Steiner resides with her partner and co-author, Lynn Adams, and is a lifelong reader and writer of horror, science fiction, and fantasy. Her short story "The Being Game" appeared in *Strained Relations* (Hypatia Press, 1989). She has also written a SF novel with Ms. Adams, which is currently making the rounds.

Karl Heinrich Ulrichs (1825–1895) was an early pioneer of the modern gay movement in Germany. He came out publicly in 1867 and, in a series of booklets from 1864 to 1879, theorized about homosexuality and defended the legal and political rights of lesbians and gay men. The results of his efforts came only after his death, however. From 1880 he lived a life of exile in Italy, and it was during this time that he published the collection *Matrosengeschichten* (Sailors' Tales), from which "Manor" was taken.

Jess Wells is the author of *Two Willow Chairs*, short fiction, and *The Dress/The Sharda Stories*, short fiction and erotica, both by Library B Books. She is currently finishing her first novel. "Succubus" first appeared in *The Dress/The Sharda Stories.*

Eric Garber is the co-author (with Lyn Paleo) of *Uranian Worlds: A Guide to Alternative Sexuality in Science Fiction, Fantasy, and Horror* (second edition; G.K. Hall, 1990) and the co-editor (with Camilla Decarnin and Lyn Paleo) of *Worlds Apart: An Anthology of Lesbian and Gay Science Fiction and Fantasy* (Alyson, 1986). He has written for *Out/Look, The Advocate, Lambda Book Report,* and *The Dictionary of Literary Biography.* He lives in San Francisco with his partner, Jeff, and their dog, Rosie.

Other books of interest from
ALYSON PUBLICATIONS

WORLDS APART, edited by Camilla Decarnin, Eric Garber, and Lyn Paleo, $8.00. The world of science fiction allows writers to freely explore alternative sexualities. These eleven stories take full advantage of that opportunity as they voyage into the futures that could await us. The authors of these stories explore issues of sexuality and gender relations in the context of futuristic societies. *Worlds Apart* challenges us by showing us our alternatives.

STEAM, by Jay B. Laws, $10.00. A vaporous presence is slowly invading San Francisco. One by one, selected gay men are seduced by it — then they disappear, leaving only a ghoulish reminder of their existence. Can anyone stop this shapeless terror?

SOMEWHERE IN THE NIGHT, by Jeffrey N. McMahan, $8.00. The realms of nightmare and reality converge in eight tales of suspense and the supernatural. Jeffrey N. McMahan weaves eerie stories with just the right amount of horror, humor, and eroticism.

VAMPIRES ANONYMOUS, by Jeffrey McMahan, $8.00. Andrew, the wry vampire, was introduced in *Somewhere in the Night,* which won the author a Lambda Literary Award. Now Andrew is back, as he confronts an organization that has already lured many of his kin from their favorite recreation, and that is determined to deprive him of the nourishment he needs for survival.

CHROME, by George Nader, $8.00. It is death to love a robot. But in their desert training ground, Chrome and King Vortex are forming a forbidden bond that could lead to intergalactic warfare.

KINDRED SPIRITS, edited by Jeffrey M. Elliot, $7.00. Twelve writers present very different images of what it could mean to be gay or lesbian in other worlds and other times.

THE WANDERGROUND, by Sally Miller Gearhart, $9.00. Gearhart's stories imaginatively portray a future women's culture, combining a control of mind and matter with a sensuous adherence to their own realities.

SUPPORT YOUR LOCAL BOOKSTORE

Most of the books described above are available at your nearest gay or feminist bookstore, and many of them will be available at other bookstores. If you can't get these books locally, order by mail using the form below.

Enclosed is $_____ for the following books. (Add $1.00 postage when ordering just one book. If you order two or more, we'll pay the postage.)

1. _____

2. _____

3. _____

name: _____

address: _____

city: _____ state: _____ zip: _____

ALYSON PUBLICATIONS
Dept. H-67, 40 Plympton St., Boston, MA 02118

After December 31, 1992, please write for current catalog.